I. H Leney

Shadowland in Ellan Vannin

Or, folk tales of the Isle of Man

I. H Leney

Shadowland in Ellan Vannin
Or, folk tales of the Isle of Man

ISBN/EAN: 9783337344825

Printed in Europe, USA, Canada, Australia, Japan

Cover: Foto ©Andreas Hilbeck / pixelio.de

More available books at **www.hansebooks.com**

SHADOWLAND

IN

ELLAN VANNIN;

OR,

𝕱olk 𝕿ales of the 𝕴sle of 𝕸an.

BY

I. H. LENEY

(MRS. J. W. RUSSELL).

LONDON:
ELLIOT STOCK, 62, PATERNOSTER ROW.
1890.

CONTENTS.

PAGE

OFF MAUGHOLD HEAD - - - - I

THE LEGEND OF ST. MICHAEL'S ISLE - - 55

THE MAGIC KIERN ROD : OR, CUR SHEN SHA IN

    GILLEY GLASH - - - - - 103

THE PHYNODDEREE, OR GOOD-NATURED FAIRY - 133

CONCLUDING CHAPTER OF SHADOWLAND IN ELLAN

    VANNIN - - - - - - 139

INTRODUCTION.

As folk-lore has for so long been thought worthy to hold a prominent position in our literature, it is surprising no patriotic Manxman has come forward to preserve the many weird and fanciful histories, fairy legends, and tales, with which his native isle abounds.

Certainly this island, with its lovely scenery, its hills and secluded glens, its rocky coast, intersected here and there with deep and picturesque caverns, gives suitable locale for fairies, elves, and water-sprites, both malignant and benign. Whilst the sonorous roar of the waves, as they beat against the shore in the drear winter time ; the soft sighing of the summer breeze, that might be the faint echo of the mermaid's song, well combine to tempt the imagination to stray into the regions of fancy, and to bring

to mind some of the strange and often poetic
ideas of former years, when it was held there was
so intimate a connection between nature and the
human race that portents of good or ill might be
drawn from every passing change in earth and air and
sky, and even the simple wayside flowers had their
tale to tell.

A few of the folk-tales of this interesting isle I have
put together in this volume, but have not, except in
the concluding chapter, followed the example of some
writers on, or compilers of, folk-lore, who give in
bare detail what they have to relate. I have en-
deavoured to introduce the superstitious beliefs and
observances that have existed, or do still exist, in
the island, clothed in the embellishment of a story,
and introducing, therefore, persons and scenes both
imaginary and drawn from the life, hoping by this
means to bring before the reader not only their tradi-
tions, but also the Manx people themselves—their
home-life, character, habits, and surroundings. Neither
have I undertaken the labour of comparing any of
these folk-tales with those of other countries. This
subject has been exhaustively gone into by so many
well-known and clever writers, who not only point
out the similarities to be found in the legendary lore

of various peoples, but in many cases trace, or pro-
fess to trace, these legends to their fountain-head.
The tales in connection with Peel Castle and Castle
Rushen, as they are already in print, and to be found
in every Isle of Man guide-book, I have not reproduced in the present volume, which I now venture to
launch forth on the wide sea of literature, knowing
that it will drift to a friendly shore, where the adverse
winds of criticism will touch it but gently ; for years of
experience have shown me not only how beautiful
and full of interest is the little Isle of Ellan Vannin,
but also how kind and true are the Manx people,
amongst whom I am proud to number many of my
best and dearest friends.

I. H. LENEY.

Ramsey.

OFF MAUGHOLD HEAD.

CHAPTER I.

The Hibernia--Eccentric landlady—Cecil Morton meets the
Parkers—Mr. Parker senior's strange tale of 'second sight'
—A ghostly female.

I WAS tempted in September, 183-, to take a trip from
Whitehaven in a fishing vessel crossing to the Isle of
Man. I had often heard of it as remarkable for the
salubrity of its climate, beautiful land and sea views,
good fishing; and what concerned me more, as I was
something of an antiquarian, that it had some very
interesting Druidical remains.

We landed at Ramsey, where I decided to settle
for a week or so. I got comfortable lodgings in a
house near the shore. I went off each day on long
excursions, sometimes with sketching materials, but
more often with my rod and fishing-tackle, getting
back at night usually pretty well tired.

One of these days, whilst fishing at a place called
Ballaglass, I was caught in so severe a thunderstorm,
followed by such deluging rain, that I had to seek

1—2

shelter at an inn that, luckily for me, was just at the entrance to the glen. As the rain continued, and the now leaden-looking sky seemed to portend a storm of no ordinary violence, I made up my mind, if they could accommodate me, to remain for the night where I was. The landlady was very civil, but at once told me that, though she could provide me with a bed, the private sitting-room I had asked for was out of the question. When I further inquired about the possibilities of dinner, her voice assumed the loud key, and her face the expression of intense surprise.

'Is it dinner yer askin' for this time? Why, it's jus' four! Lord bless the lad! It's tea or supper yer meanin', surely?'

'Well, call it whatever you like, my good woman, but give me something to eat.'

'Won't bread an' cheese an' a good glass of beer serve ye?' she asked, glancing at me out of the corner of her keen, rather deep-set eyes.

She was an odd figure, certainly, dressed in a blue petticoat of some sort of cloth or flannel, surmounted by a man's pilot-jacket, a good deal too long in the sleeves; to obviate the inconvenience this would have caused the cuffs were turned back, displaying a pair of large muscular-looking hands and wrists, quite out of proportion to her size, as she was considerably below the middle height.

'Well, won't that do for ye?' for I did not immediately reply.

' I must make bread and cheese do if you can give me nothing else.'

' Well, I'll give ye a fresh-laid egg or two. Ye'll not starve, never fear; and mebbe ye'll have some fish in yer basket, an' them and a drop of good whisky to finish with, an' keep out the could, that'll do for ye, it's like? but it's here ye'll have to take it, there's nowhere else for ye.'

We were in the kitchen all this time; I was standing before the fire trying to dry my steaming clothes. There was nothing to be said against it, a comfortable enough little room, except that at present some three or four countrymen, farmers apparently, were seated there, smoking vile tobacco, drinking, and having a noisy discussion as to the prices some cattle had fetched at a recent fair. I certainly would have wished more agreeable accompaniments to my meal, than the uproar and nasty odours of blended smoke and beer.

' Is there no other room I can go to?' I asked; and just as my hostess was about to reply in the negative, a gentleman, who had entered a moment or two before, and, like myself, was drying himself at the blazing hearth, turned round and said to me with a good deal of courtesy:

' If you will join my father and me in the next room we shall be very happy. I see,' glancing at my wet things, ' that, like myself, you have been caught in this heavy storm; but you seem to have been further from shelter than I, to judge from the comparative moisture of our garments.'

I looked down at my muddy boots and damp things, and, thanking him, muttered something to the effect that I ' was not very presentable.' Here the landlady interposed :

' Oh, is that all that's doin' on ye ; I'll soon have ye dry an' tidy. Here, ye can do yer hair—it's all through-others—with this ready in' comb,' handing me the remnants of one from a table near. 'An' now sit down, and take off yer boots ; we'll soon get them dried, and cleaned, too.'

I sat down to comply, my new acquaintance looking on with an amused smile.

' Then I may expect you in about half an hour ?' he asked.

I again thanked him, and accepted, while the queer old woman attending me cried after him as he was leaving the kitchen :

' He'll be at ye directly ;' then turning to me, she said : ' Ye'll be from the other side of the water, I'm thinkin' ?'

I replied in the affirmative.

' From Liverpool, mebbe ?'

' No,' I said ; but seeing the poor old soul was full of curiosity, and feeling that I owed her some consideration for all the good offices she was performing for me, I proceeded further to tell her, ' I crossed from Whitehaven here, and I belong to London.'

'Lunnon! why, that's a terrible long way off! There was a person here last summer—he was over about the mines, an' stayin' in Ramsey; but he was in here times sittin', an' he was sayin' he come from Lunnon. It's like ye'll know him, when yer from the same place? His name was Smith.'

When I told her I had not the pleasure of Mr. Smith's acquaintance—

'Well, that's quare now, an' ye both livin' in the one town.'

At last, after a good wash in the bedroom I was to occupy for the night, and having been duly inspected by my odd landlady, who said, with an approving nod, 'Ye'll do,' I in turn asked a few questions as to her 'parlour company,' as she designated the gentlemen of whose hospitality I was about to avail myself.

She was not very warm in her commendations.

'The father's quare,' she said, touching her forehead in a significant manner; 'the other's middlin'. He goes about with th' ould man everywhere, an' they don't give much throuble, an' pay reg'lar—oh, I've no fault with them at all, at all! It seems he was here years ago when he was a young falla, an' he stopped in this very house, an' nothin' else 'll serve him but stop here agen, he will. I've nothing agin them. Ta chengey ni host ny share na olk y ghra,* ye know. Parker their name is, an' it appears the

---

* The translation, which I give below, I learned later on: 'The silent tongue is better than evil speaking.'

ould man's mother was a Manx woman. Cowen her name was, but there's Cowens an' Cowens, an' which of them *his* mother belongs to beats me. I'm thinkin' he does not know himself. On he's quare—quare enough.'

I found Mr. Parker and his son awaiting me. The former was a dignified, intellectual-looking man, with something sad in his expression, and that far-away look in the eyes that one sees sometimes with those who have passed through sorrow. His hair was snow-white, but he appeared hale and strong for his age, which he told me later in the evening was seventy-nine. The son was an unusually handsome man, of, I should have judged, forty-five or thereabouts. They introduced themselves to me as John and George Parker, coal merchants, residing a few miles out of Whitehaven, and I then handed them my card. The old gentleman started as he read it.

'Cecil Morton!' he cried, in accents expressive of the greatest surprise; 'Cecil Morton! why, how strange—how very strange! I formed a devoted schoolboy friendship with a Cecil Morton which lasted till he died, or met his end, I should say, in a most mysterious manner, in this very Island of Man. I still think of him with all the warmth of my early affection. He was some years my junior. He would be now, if living, about seventy-four or five, I should say. Could he have been any relation of yours, I wonder?'

'He must have been my uncle, my father's half-brother, after whom I was named. I have heard my mother say he was drowned ; that he was supposed to have fallen off some rocks into the sea. This happened when my father was still a boy. I did not remember though that the scene of the disaster was in the Isle of Man. My parents both died when I was a mere child. Of my father I have only a dim recollection.'

'Then you are the son of the little brother Fred, of whom my friend used to speak with so much affection. Who can say life is prosaic—without incident—when such things as this occur ?'

It certainly was a most extraordinary coincidence, and at once established us all on a more friendly footing than would probably have been arrived at in many days in the ordinary course of acquaintanceship.

'You have no resemblance to your uncle,' remarked Mr. Parker. 'He was of a good medium height ; you are, I should think, quite six feet high, and broad in proportion, whilst he was slightly formed—with pale-blue eyes and fair hair, while your eyes and hair are dark. In fact, my dear boy, you are what would be considered a very handsome man, whereas your poor uncle and namesake was only passably well-looking.'

Though I had arrived at the dignity of twenty-five years, I could not help feeling a little awkward at the old gentleman's close scrutiny and broad compliments; and his son, seeing my embarrassment, came to the rescue, saying:

'Well, father, we will now, I think, get something to eat, and after that I dare say Mr. Morton will be glad to hear anything you can tell him about his uncle.'

'Ah, well! Yes. It is even still a painful subject to me. He was murdered, and I was given warning of his fate in a most mysterious way by what is called "second sight." If only I had not allowed myself to be laughed out of regarding this warning, you might have had your uncle now, and I my friend all these years!'

Murdered! This was decidedly ghostly and chilling; but what can interfere with the healthy appetite of five-and-twenty years, a clear conscience, and a hardy constitution. I did ample justice to the good things provided by Mrs. Rachel Looney, as I found our hostess was named, and we all wound up with some of her home-brewed whisky. Mr. Parker junior, whose lively chat acted as a capital antidote to his father's melancholy reminiscences, I found a most agreeable man, and I should gladly have excused what I felt sure from the preface was going to be some ghastly history of my unknown uncle's fate; in fact, I should have preferred its being buried in oblivion as far as I was concerned. However, the room was well lighted and cheery, the cigars of mine host excellent, as might

also be said of Mrs. Rachel's home-brewed, so, under
the ameliorating circumstances of my comfortable
surroundings, I prepared for the worst. Certainly, we
had in the howlings of the storm, with occasional vivid
flashes of lightning, a suitable accompaniment for the
weirdest of ghost stories or of second sight ; and the
old man, with his deep voice and melancholy, im-
pressive manner, gave great dramatic effect to the
recital.

'You, of course, are not aware,' he began, ' that my
mother was a Manx woman.'

I did not think it necessary to tell him that I was
already informed on this subject, but let him proceed
uninterrupted :

' My father was English—a Liverpool man, captain
of a merchant vessel trading to South America. I
was the only child, and, by my mother's wish, was
sent for education to Mr. ——'s school, in Douglas
—going home for my Christmas holidays; the Mid-
summer ones I spent with my grandmother at Maughold. I had been about two years at this school,
when a new boarder, a delicate, timid boy, came from
London. Some of the lads, who, I must say, were
bullies, took advantage of his gentle disposition, and
he would have been very badly used sometimes if I
had not constituted myself his champion. There is
no need now to enter into the whys and the where-
fores of my having sufficient influence to befriend him,
or give details of our lives during those school-days,

or trace the growth and steadiness of our friendship. It is all so far back it could not possibly have any interest for you. I shall, therefore, at once come to the time when Cecil and I, men of twenty-eight and twenty-three respectively, again visited the island. We put up at this very inn. I was not then blessed with too much of this world's goods. Your uncle was rich, and very careless in letting it be seen how well he was provided with money, and also in carrying rather large sums about on his person. He was something of a naturalist, and used to go rambling over the country hunting up specimens of insects, birds, and so on. I took no interest in these pursuits, and could not always accompany him, as my grandmother was very ill with what, in fact, proved to be her last illness. I used to have to spend a great part of my time attending to her, as she liked having me with her. She lodged with some kindly people at Maughold, and had no near relatives living—my mother, who was her last surviving child, had died two years before. You will say this is irrelevant, but I only go into these details to let you know why I did not always accompany my friend on his expeditions. One night I had been kept very late with my grandmother. It was getting on for midnight when I prepared to take the road from Maughold to the inn here. It was a fine October night, the moon shining brightly, so I did not mind the walk.

‘ “ Cecil will be uneasy,” I thought, as I started,

" at my being so late, though probably he will conjecture the cause."

' I walked on briskly till I arrived at a place where, on my left, lay a small bay, between two bold headlands. I paused a moment, arrested by the beauty of the scene. The sea stretched far beyond, glittering in the clear rays shed by the Queen of Night, calm and peaceful as far as eye could reach, except where, here and there, it came swirling up in white spray against some jagged, dark-looking rocks that impeded its progress to the shore. As I gazed I was suddenly startled by hearing just behind me the sound of a heavy sigh, and, turning, I beheld the figure of a woman, clothed in long clinging black garments. Her face was invisible, as over it she had some covering, semi-transparent, but too thick for my eyes to penetrate in the uncertain light. I was so taken by surprise that for a moment I did nothing but stare at the strange apparition. She looked, to use a Scotch phrase, " so uncanny," at that hour, and in that solitary place.

' " A beautiful night," I took courage to remark, though, I must confess, in a rather quavering voice.

' For all reply she turned to me for a second, and, giving a moan so heart-broken, so unearthly, I shuddered to hear, then, wringing her hands, she glided rapidly away towards the sea, and I presently saw her ascending—it could not be called climbing—a high rock that jutted far out into the water and adjoined the nearest headland.

' "She is going to drown herself, poor wretched creature !" I exclaimed.

' I at once dashed after her, dreading lest I should not be in time to prevent this self-murder. I scaled as rapidly as I could the slippery rocks beneath those on which she was standing, her tall, dark-robed figure showing in bold relief against the bright shimmering water, but looking more like part of the eminence on which she stood than a living human being.

' "If she sees me," I thought, " she may hasten matters, and throw herself down before I can get to her."

' After many falls and numberless cuts and bruises, I reached a more secure foothold. To my surprise and relief, the woman, just as I arrived here, turned, and, with the same gliding motion that she had ascended to it, came down from her elevated position, passed beneath where I stood, disappeared for a few seconds under the shadow of the rising ground, and, in less time than I can take to relate it, was far above me on the headland, and making, with extraordinary rapidity, for the precipitous cliffs leading to Maughold Head. Some strong impulse—curiosity, or anxiety to prevent suicide—but what feeling I cannot define, impelled me to follow and see the end of this strange adventure. On in front I could still discern the lithe figure threading her way from one steep point to another. Once or twice she paused in her dangerous progress, and looked back, as if to ascertain whether I

was following, and at last, to my intense dismay, she
suddenly disappeared, whilst a shriek so awful as, even
after this interval of years, makes me shudder as I
recall it, rang out upon the silence of the night.   I
rushed madly forward, and prepared to make as rapid
a descent as was possible of the steep decline from
which I concluded the unfortunate creature had thrown
herself, when I was arrested and, as it were, held spell-
bound by strains of the most exquisite music, that
seemed coming in softest breathings from hills, and
sea, and shore, as though many different instruments
were blended into harmony by the gently moving air
around ; and then, clear and sweet above all, sung, as
it were, in childish treble, sounded the words :

> ' " Stranger, stranger, come not near ;
> Court not death ; descend not here."

I stood immovable — fear lost in astonishment and
the delight of listening to such sounds ; but as they
got fainter and fainter, and at last ceased, borne away
on the soft breezes that had played about me, I awoke
to the consciousness that I was on haunted ground ;
and with this consciousness came a feeling of terror,
that, though I longed to fly, yet, as in some dreadful
nightmare, my feet seemed rooted to the spot, and I
was compelled to be a horror-struck spectator of a
scene to me so heartrending, so awful——'

Mr. Parker paused, seemingly overcome by merely
recalling it all ; and only that I was doubtful how it

might be received, I would have suggested his giving up, or, at all events, postponing the narration of what was evidently so painful to him.   I glanced at Parker junior, hoping he might propose a respite ; but he was absorbed apparently in the enjoyment of his cigar and his own thoughts, and either quite indifferent on the subject, or unobservant of his father's state of agitation and my boredom.

I looked upon the whole thing—the mysterious warning, music, haunted ground, ghostly female—as the mere outcome of a diseased or over-excited brain, and decided that Mrs. Looney had good grounds for her assertion that 'th' ould man was quare !'

CHAPTER II.

Mr. Parker's horrible vision of his friend's murder.

AFTER awhile Mr. Parker had very much recovered himself, and in a calmer voice continued his recital :

'I told you that I saw all that I have related to you so far in the clear light of a very bright moon ; for the sky was unobscured, except where here and there clouds that looked more like snow-wreaths than anything else floated in the ambient air. But scarcely had the echo of that dreadful scream been stilled, when stealing along the waters from the far horizon spread a gray, cold mist, and with it came the dull, moaning sound of rising wind ; whilst white-winged sea-mews flew with frightened cries towards land. The water beat with low, angry sound against the rocks beneath, and still this threatening rain-cloud widened and rolled on, darker and denser each moment, till all was enveloped in its chilly folds. The landscape, the shore and cliffs beneath, the very ground on which I stood, was hidden from my sight. I trembled as it crept round me—my eyeballs ached, my pulses throbbed, my breath came short, and, in

2

gasps in the ice-cold air, I cursed my folly for ven-
turing on such dangerous heights; whilst all the many
tales with which my grandmother used to regale my
childish ears—of pixies, fairies, water-sprites, and
ghosts—that I had since laughed at as old-world
superstitions, forced themselves unpleasantly on my
mind; for I could not for a moment doubt that I was
under a weird spell, cast round me by some supernatural agency.   But what and by whom was I influenced—for good or for ill?   Was the woman a
phantom, sent to lure me to destruction?   Whilst
pondering thus, unable to move, and even, if I had
not been deprived of any power of volition, to stir
from the spot on which I was might have been almost
instant death, for I knew that beneath me yawned
that fearful precipice—well, as I was about to say,
whilst I was shivering with cold, and fear, and dread
as to how all this might end, the oppression on my
chest seemed gradually to lessen.   I breathed more
freely; the tension on brain and muscles relaxed.
My eyes, which I had kept closed for some time, I
slowly and gradually opened, and great indeed was
my astonishment at what now met my view.   The
dull, gray cloud was fast disappearing, and instead of
the moonlight that had first lit up the scene, the
whole landscape was being rapidly illuminated in the
bright, red glow of an autumn sunset.   I can com-
pare the whole thing to nothing so well as the transi-
tion-scene in a theatre.   In my normal state I should,

of course, have known that all these sudden meta-
morphoses in nature could not by possibility be
occurring. But I was under some wonderful mesmeric
influence, controlled and acted upon by a will to
which my own was for the time completely sub-
servient; and as the dense pall that had veiled everything floated away in the distance, tinted by the
ruddy glare that tipped the headlands and tinged
everywhere it reached with the hue of blood, I
seemed to succumb more and more, to be oblivious
of time, friends, all sense of danger—in fact, of my
very existence. The powers of my mind, my brain,
were absorbed in watching the tragedy that was presented to the eyes of my "inner sense." Apropos of
that inner sense I allude to, I hope I shall on some
future occasion have an opportunity of going more
fully into it, and explaining my views on the subject
to you.'

I bowed whilst uttering a polite 'Thank you; I
hope so.' Mentally, I determined, as far as I could
prevent it, that opportunity should never occur.

'You must remember,' he continued, 'that I
believed all I am about to describe to you to be
actually happening; otherwise you could not understand the agony I endured.

'I shall now proceed, and I trust calmly (it is all
so many years ago), with the rest of this strange
vision, and what next presented itself to me. Just
beneath, as if poised in mid-air—so perpendicular

and steep was the cliff, so narrow the path on which he stood — was my friend Cecil Morton carefully threading his way step by step, and holding on now and again to some overhanging branch or bracken. There was nothing in this to make me tremble for his safety. He was from constant habit an expert climber, sure-footed, and had a steady head. He used frequently to scale just such giddy heights, hunting after sea-birds who make their home in almost inaccessible places ; but what turned me cold, and made my heart stand still with sickening dread, was that stealthily and closely following was a man— a fiend in human shape. He carried in his hand some heavy weapon, raised ready to strike the unconscious Cecil down. Had Morton turned and seen his danger, he could not have averted the blow, or saved himself ; he could not even have grappled with his foe—any backward movement in the effort to defend himself would have precipitated him on the rocks below. Of the murderous intent of the man there could be no doubt. You can imagine the intensity of my suffering when seeing the peril of my friend, believing all to be real, and yet being quite incapable of rendering help. I could not even raise my voice in warning. The blow I dreaded fell ; and, O God ! I live over again the torture of that moment as I stood powerless and saw Cecil's form sway for half a second, and then fall—fall—from that dreadful cliff to the rocky shore beneath. There he lay, stiff and motionless, to all appearance *dead.* The wretch who had done the deed first looked round in all directions, scanning the heights on which I was standing, but evidently without being made aware of my presence ; for, seemingly satisfied there had been no witness to his awful crime, he cautiously com-menced his descent to where his victim lay—no easy matter, I could see. He clung now and again to a piece of jutting rock or boulder, and often nearly slipped as some of the brittle ground gave way under his weight. Many a time as I watched, a wild hope that I might see him hurled to the bottom sprang up within my mind. He arrives at last at the top of a piece of slaty rock where no foothold can be found. How will he manage now? For a moment he seems puzzled, and looks round as if in the hope of finding some place more easy to scale ; but everywhere within his reach nothing is to be seen but the same smooth, unbroken, nearly perpendicular surface. He hesitates no longer ; but, straightening his limbs, and holding his arms closely to his sides, he lets himself slide down the declivity, arriving safely on the smooth gravel beneath. After arranging his garments, and removing from them all traces of his rapid descent, he walked (and I, for the first time, perceived he had a slight limp) to where his victim lay, and at once proceeded to discover whether life was extinct and his foul purpose accomplished. Having satisfied himself on this point, he began hastily to rifle the body. I could see him convey the watch, purse, and a lot of loose notes and gold from Morton's person to his own. He then walked away round a tiny clump of rocks, and was hidden from my view for a short space of time. " He intends," I thought, "hiding the body in some cave, or burying it under the sand and gravel"—a better chance of concealment than if thrown into the sea, where any passing boat might pick up the corpse, ere he would have sufficient time to effect his escape.

' The sound of the dip of oars drew my attention to the point where the murderer had been lost to my sight ; the next moment he pulled up into the bay or inlet, and, securing the boat to a wooden pile—one of several—he got on to the beach, and, going over to the side of the murdered man, lifted up the lifeless body, and, throwing it into the bottom of the boat, hastily covered it over with some old sails, and pulled rapidly away from land.

' As I followed the movements of the boat, I saw for the first time, pretty far out to sea, a small fishing-lugger. For this the man seemed to be making. " He has an accomplice or accomplices," I decided. I kept my eyes fixed on the fast-receding boat, but I was not destined to see more, for again one of those extra-ordinary changes set in. The unnatural brightness of the horizon was clouded over, the sunlight faded swiftly away into the gray haze of a clouded winter day, and gradually, sweeping so close to the water, as almost to seem a part of its depths, came the same heavy mist. Everything was hidden from me for a brief space; but as quickly as it had come—as quickly did it disappear. I opened my eyes—which I had for a few moments involuntarily closed—to find myself on the same spot where I had stopped to admire the beautiful Bay of Corna, and where I had first seen the black-draped woman. How I had made my way back I cannot tell——'

'Dreamt it all,' interrupted Mr. George Parker laconically.

'Dreamt it!' repeated the old man, in indignant tones; 'then, how do you account for all that afterwards occurred to confirm the truth of the vision?'

'I fancy that, although you were not conscious of it, you often experienced a good deal of anxiety about your friend in his dangerous feats of climbing, and perhaps had an undefined dread he ran risks of being robbed and murdered, carrying, as you were aware, so much money about his person. People's minds are more occupied with, and affected by, outward events, oftentimes, than they realize themselves. The accidents and circumstances, many of them, of daily life that we may consider trivial, and the ideas produced by them as only evanescent, are yet sufficiently fixed on the brain as to be reproduced in dreams. Besides all this, you had a very fatiguing time with your grandmother, often losing your proper modicum of sleep, to brace you up for your walk from her place to the inn;

you had probably partaken of some glasses of hot toddy, which would possibly induce drowsiness, and, resting to admire the view, you had fallen asleep, and dreamed a most thrilling and remarkable dream. As to all that happened afterwards, as if in confirmation of your vision—look how many strange coincidences occur quite naturally in real life, without any supernatural agency being at work. You, therefore——'

'Pray cease; do not repeat this nonsense, George!' cried his father so angrily that I interposed, to stop what I feared might terminate in an angry discussion, by asking, 'And about the woman, sir; what of her?'

'The woman! oh! yes—but I had not nearly told you all' ('Good Heavens!' thought I, 'midnight will not see us in bed'), 'when my son thought proper to interrupt me, with his absurd attempts at explaining what can *never* be explained.'

'Suppose, then, father,' Mr. George said, smiling good-humouredly, 'we adjourn this meeting for to-night, and get a promise from Mr. Morton that he will breakfast with us to-morrow morning, and join us in the evening at dinner, or supper, as Mrs. Looney insists on calling our six o'clock meal.'

This kind invitation was gladly accepted by me. I felt very sleepy, and hailed with delight the near prospect of getting to bed, and was heartily glad to say good-night to my hosts and the elder one's ghastly reminiscences.

CHAPTER III

Mistress Looney's 'Pegasus,' and how she mounted him—More
of Mr. Parker's experiences—Mrs. Cowen's death.

THE next morning we were up betimes. Whilst seated
at breakfast, the eccentric landlady* put her head in
at the door.

'I hard ye,' she said, looking at me, 'sayin' las'
night that ye'd have to go t' Ramsey to tell the pesson
yer lodgin' with that yer safe-t, an' for to get some
clothes. I'm goin' to town meself, an' I'll give her
yer message, an' fetch back yer bit duds, if ye put a
word or two on a bit of paper sayin' what yer wantin'
like. It's a fine day for fishin' afther th' rain, not too
bright, so you an' Masther George can go yer ways
together an' see what'll ye catch. I'll put ye some-
thin' to eat in yer basket—an' ye'll be back for supper,
for six.'

I thanked the old woman, as I handed her the
'written word or two,' and then inquired if she was

---

* This odd person is a real character, accurately portrayed
from description given to the author by people who had known
her.

driving, as otherwise the parcel would be too heavy
for her.

'Ye'll get it right enough—never fear,' she said
rather shortly, and left the room.

'Masther George,' as she called him, bade me
turn my attention to the window. I looked out and
saw a large raw-boned cart-horse (by its build and
the long fetlocks I should judge it so). What did
duty for a saddle was a bag or sack thrown across the
animal's back, from which straw might be seen stick-
ing out here and there, proclaiming the nature of the
padding. Presently Mrs. Looney's voice sounded out,
loud and shrill, giving parting orders. I then saw her
come out, dressed exactly as on the previous day,
except that this morning her head was surmounted
by a man's hat of rough beaver, instead of the sun-
bonnet. She, with the assistance of an uncouth-look-
ing stable-boy, briskly mounted her steed, seating
herself astride, in manly fashion,* and giving her
Pegasus a slight touch with a switch she carried, was
soon riding at a fair pace towards Ramsey.

'Mrs. Looney rarely travels a distance any other
way,' said old Mr. Parker, who was amused at my
surprise.

That evening, after a successful day's fishing and
an excellent dinner, we got out pipes and cigars and
settled ourselves comfortably as on the previous night.

* It is a fact that the landlady of the Hibernia, about whom
the author writes, used to perform journeys in this way.

I was fondly hoping I should escape the rest of the old gentleman's unpleasant histories ; but no ! I saw him getting ready, and with a few preliminary ' hems ' and clearing of the voice he began. I had decided I need not listen, as he talked without pause or expecting any comment on what he was relating ; but, spite of myself, I was carried along with the story, and, probably from being less tired than last night, found myself following with interest the rest of the strange tale :

'I left off — if my memory serves me right — at where I found myself again standing at the spot where I had paused to look at the Bay of Corna.

'I felt bewildered—ill—the horror of all that had been shown me still oppressed me. I was roused by a sudden intense anxiety about my friend. We had parted immediately after breakfast—I to take the cross-road to Maughold village, and he intended starting soon after me for Ramsey, where he would get a sailing-boat and make for the Head, and there, he said, he would put ashore.

' "Don't go in for any of your foolhardy climbing," I advised.

' "I won't promise that," he responded, as he waved me an adieu.

' Remembering all this, after my dreadful vision, a sickening fear seized me, lest some evil had befallen him. I made all possible haste homewards, and who could describe the joy, the thankfulness, I felt when, on nearing the inn, I saw Cecil standing at the door, and evidently looking out for me.

'"I had just begun to think you were not coming; but, dear me ! what is the matter?" he exclaimed, as I drew near enough for him to see my face. "Is the poor granny worse? or—or——"

'"She is not worse now," I managed to say; but the reaction had proved too much for me, and for the first time in my life I fainted dead away. When I came to, I found I was in this little parlour. Morton had managed to drag me in on to the rug. I was very wet from having had the contents of a large jug of water poured over me, and just escaped a second bath by so opportunely opening my eyes.

'"Now, then, drink this brandy and water, and off to bed," said Cecil commandingly. "Not a word !" as I prepared to speak. "Here, up with you! Now take my arm."

'I felt too ill to resist; but before bidding him good-night, I begged he would not go out in the morning without first seeing me.

'"Not likely I should do so, my dear Parker, after your wonderful exploit of fainting just now."

'As he was quitting my room, he turned round to say :

'"I shall put a veto upon such a close attendance upon poor Mrs. Cowen."

'The next morning I rose quite well and refreshed, after a good sleep, and was inclined then to take much the same view as my son now does of the warning of the previous night; and when I at breakfast related the whole thing to Morton, he laughed heartily, and said:

' "You probably dreamt it all in a few minutes. Did you know the time when your adventures began, and when they ended? We might go and look for the ghostly woman's body, supposing she was the happy possessor of such a thing? I must not have anything to do with a boatman with dark, scowling countenance, especially if he limps," etc.

'Not only had I to endure unlimited "chaff" from Morton, but when later on we both went into Ramsey, he related my "nightmare," as he called it, to several of our acquaintances that we met there: one and all laughed me out of any serious thoughts of my previous night's "supposed adventures."

'Ah, me! but one short week had passed when I viewed it all very differently.

'The day I am now going to tell you of Cecil had started with me, after our early breakfast, for Maughold, he for the express purpose of looking for some sea-birds, or their eggs—I forget which; I am, and always have been, an ignoramus about everything connected with natural history—I, of course, was bound for Mrs. Cowen's.

'The morning was misty, and a fog seemed sweeping from the sea.

' "You will not, of course, go after birds in such

hazy weather as this," I asked, as we were parting at
my grandmother's door.

' "Oh, certainly not !" he replied.   "If it does not
improve, I shall get Mac to row me into Ramsey,
and I can then look up the Moores, and the rest—pay
a few calls, in fact : for I won't have much time, as I
have to start from here in so few days."

' "And who is Mac ?"

' " Mac !   Don't you know him ?—though I believe
he told me he is a new-comer.   He and his wife
live in that little thatched cottage you have to pass
every time you come to or from here, just before you
turn on to the beach at Corna.   He is an Irishman,
but married, I understand, to a Manx woman.   She
looks wretched enough, poor creature !   I feel con-
vinced he's a brute to her—not that she would admit
it.   She's an apt illustration of—you know the
proverb : something about a woman, a dog, and a
walnut-tree, 'The more you beat 'em, the better they'll
be.'   I'm sure he follows this advice, for she often has
queer marks about the eyes and face, but seems
devoted to the man.   He's got her well in hand."

' " And why do you employ such a monster ?"

' " Simply, my dear fellow, that, besides the wife, he
has a boat—the only one to be had on hire in this
neighbourhood—and I find it most convenient when-
ever I 'take the notion,' as they say here, of being
rowed into Ramsey, to get him and the aforesaid boat
to take me.   Ta-ta !"

'We parted; and I was never to see him in life again!

'The mist, instead of passing off, seemed to become denser. I remained at the cottage with my poor suffering relative till the afternoon, when I thought it would be time to rejoin my friend, who had said he would be back about six. As I was wending my way to the inn, there came on a sudden darkening of the horizon, which seemed to portend a storm. A dense fog set in, spreading far into shore, and completely hiding the landscape. I knew my way so well, or I should have been rather puzzled how to proceed, so thick did this mist become. I could hear the shrill cry of the sea-gulls, and there was a low, sobbing sound in the faint breeze that was stirring, like coming rain.

'I quickened my steps, fearing a drenching; but after this strange blackness over the heavens a change set in : the mist receded gradually from the land, and at last faded away. By the time I had got to the highroad, and near my destination, a bright red illumined the sky; the clouds, lately so black or leaden gray, were tinged with rosy light.

'Your uncle, I found, had not returned, but I felt no uneasiness on this account, as I concluded some of his friends in Ramsey had kept him ; so I sat down to the evening meal alone. At last, when ten o'clock struck, I began to feel anxious. I passed another hour, feeling more and more uncomfortable ; and my "vision" or "nightmare" came unpleasantly into my thoughts, as it flashed quickly upon me how like had the almost phenomenal changes in the atmosphere of this day been to what I witnessed in my—dream, shall I call it? I could no longer remain inactive. I decided to go into the town, late as it was. I should most probably meet my friend on his return journey. The night was dark, so I borrowed a lantern from the good people at the inn, telling them at the same time where I was going, and that I did not expect to be long, as I should most likely meet Mr. Morton on the way.

'On and on I went; but no Cecil. "I shall find him at the Moores', no doubt, playing whist, or singing duets with Miss Mary; and for a moment the colour mounted to my face, as I thought what fun that merry girl, assisted by Morton, would make of me for my needless anxiety—"needless, please God," I whispered, and thought I could well sustain the ridicule, if only my friend was safe. "It is that beastly dream that frightens me, and that only; there is no real cause for apprehension," I tried to persuade myself.

'I went first to the Moores', but found the house in darkness. They were evidently all in bed, so I went on to several of our bachelor friends, whom I found still up. None of them had seen Morton.

'Wilson, a very good-natured young fellow, who seemed to think I had sufficient grounds for anxiety, suggested that your uncle might, perhaps, be sleeping at the Moores', as neither he or any whom I had met had seen him. I hoped this might be the case, though it was a very forlorn hope, as he had hitherto been particular always to be back in good time at night. After some hesitation I returned to the Moores'—accompanied by Wilson—knocked loudly two or three times to no purpose, but the fourth peal had an effect : an upper window was opened.

' " Who's there ? What's the matter ?" cried the voice of the " head of the family."

' After due explanation on my part, and apologies also, I was assured by Mr. Moore that Morton had not been at his place that day ; or, indeed, in Ramsey at all, he thought. This was very bad news for me ; and though I had pressing invitations from him and other friends to remain the night, I firmly declined. I was all impatience now to get back to the inn, so I retraced my steps, Wilson good - naturedly coming part of the way with me.

' Arrived at home, I saw a light cart at the door, and my landlord, holding a lantern, peering down the road in the direction in which I was coming.

' " Here he is !" he cried, as he spied me.

' " Is Mr. Morton back ?" I called out.

' " No, sir, he is'n ; but Misthress Cowen is took much worse. It's not thought she'll put through the night ; an' theere's a lad here, with a cart at him, to dhrive ye to Maughold."

'What a night of trouble and anxiety this was
proving! And as I sat beside the boy in the shaky
vehicle, behind a fat mare, that nothing would either
persuade or compel to get beyond an awkward "jog-
trot," I had ample time in which to be miserable; and
certainly the opportunity was not lost. Beside the sorrow
I was feeling for my dear grandmother, the gloomy
night and all combined to fill me with the most
anxious and depressing forebodings about my friend.

'"Ah, my lad! my dear boy! so you're there. I
was watching for you," the poor old lady cried as I
entered. She had just come out of one of those dis-
tressing attacks of almost suffocation that was the
hardest to endure, and the most painful symptom to
witness of her complaint. How patiently these
paroxysms were borne by her, sustained by a strength
and submission marvellous to behold! When I
expressed pity, she would say, gently laying her hand
on mine:

'"My boy, there's a 'needs be,' or it would not
be sent me; and should I not rejoice in that I am
partaker of His sufferings?"

'"How are you, granny?" I asked. Alas, I hardly
need have done so! Already the cold dews of death
were gathering on her brow.

'"My dear lad," and her voice was wonderfully
strong, the end so close at hand—"yes, dear boy, I
am nearing the 'haven of rest — the haven of rest!'
I can almost see the land that is illumined by the

rays shed from the Sun of Righteousness—no earth clouds between. Ay, ay! it will soon be for me 'no longer through a glass darkly,' but ' face to face.' I shall ' see my precious Saviour—*face to face !*' Already 'joy unspeakable' fills my soul!" She paused a moment, her countenance radiant with a light that was not of earth.

Presently she tried to turn towards me. The nurse gently moved the pillow.

'" Take my hand, vien," she said, "and never forget that, sooner or later, as the Lord wills, you will have to lie, as you see me now, at the point of death. See, dear lad, that you never forget this. You are young still, and the life I am leaving behind—the earth life—is still before you, in which you can choose ' the evil or the good.' You will have your share of sorrow and your share of joy, times of anxiety and times of peace; but never lose faith. Look up to the loving Saviour, always, always, in thankfulness for mercies and blessings bestowed, resignation and perfect trust, when disappointment or trouble visit you, as they will, dear boy,—ay, indeed! and temptations; but be strong to resist in the power of His might, for we are told we shall be helped to overcome—that 'there's a way to escape.' I am praying for you, that you may ever follow the guidings of the Holy Spirit."

' Again she paused. I stooped and kissed the dear hand I held, my eyes dim with unshed tears.

'" You're sorry for your granny, dear, and you'll

come in whiles, when you can, and put a flower, may-be, on her grave where she'll be laid, in Maughold Churchyard.   There's where your grandfather, too, was buried, as you know.   You'll not remember him well. Ah, my dear husband! my man! my John!—you were called after him, John Cowen.   Ay, indeed, we put through rough seas together, and sailed o'er smooth, he and I, but we were happy with each other! ay, *very!*   Times I would fret when things went wrong, and think the rough waves were driving us on to hard, pitiless rocks, to wreck ; and now I can look back and see how all these things that seemed to our blind judg-ment 'contrary winds' were meant to bring us at last to the shores of the eternal kingdom."

'Her voice was gradually getting weaker ; she ceased addressing me, and I could see her lips moving in silent prayer.   Again she spoke, but only by bend-ing close could I catch what she said :

'"You're here, Johnnie ?"

'"Yes, dear granny."

'"I can hardly see now ; the eyes of—the earth body—are closing—lad—that the eyes of the spiritual may—be—for ever opened—when I shall behold— 'the King in His beauty.'   The parson's not here, Johnnie ?"

'"No, grandmother."

'"He was here, though."

'"Would you wish for him ?   He has only gone a short time.   Shall I send for him ?"

' " No—no."

'She then lay so still that the nurse, who was at the other side of the bed, and I both thought for a moment that she had passed away. Suddenly her eyes opened, and, gazing beyond me, her face lighted up with a strange rapture, she freed herself from my clasp, and stretching out both her hands, she cried :

' " John, John, you here ? my darling ! my husband ! Take my hands ; hold them, dear. I had a dreadful dream, John—that we were parted—and ay! but I was longing—longing terrible—but we are together now— God be praised ! Ay, indeed, I was wearying for you ; and now we are hand in hand, never to part—never— to—part."

'The momentary strength gave way; the shade of death passed over the countenance, so radiant but one second before ! The kind, loving friend of my child-hood, of all my life, was gone from me !

' And as I gazed at the dear face that had always had a ready smile for me now lying so still in that mysterious sleep, the white lids shading the blue eyes that would never again in this world be bent on me with looks of love, of sympathy—how far away she seemed !—the full realization of all I had lost rushed upon me with overwhelming force, and the pent-up tears flowed freely. Yes, yes, I was little more than a boy then, and I am now a very old man, but I remember it all ; yes, well—better than the things of yesterday !

CHAPTER IV.

Mr. Cecil Morton's disappearance—The McInnis—Finding of Morton's body—McInnis's death—Mistress Rachel Looney's old coins and long journey—Conclusion.

'WITH the morning light came recollection of my friend Cecil, whom, in the pain and agitation I had been passing through, I had almost forgotten. "Very likely he got back all right last night to the inn, or else will return this morning," I tried to persuade myself, but could not shake off my fears as to his safety; and, early as it was, I determined to send to the inn to inquire if they had had any intelligence. I accordingly summoned Mrs. Quayle.

' "Sendin' now this early!" she exclaimed. "Why, there'll not be none of them up!"

' "I think I'll walk there myself; it is better than sitting here with my unhappy thoughts."

' "Go yerself! Oh no, no, sir; there's no call for that at all. I'll sen' an' willin'; only I'm thinkin' it's no manner o' use; for Thomas won't get in, it's like."

' "I would really rather go myself; the air will do me good," I added, as the kind-hearted landlady still demurred.

' "Oh, if that's how it's with ye, mebbe ye'd better take the road yerself; but ye musn' think I'm not willin' to do that an' more for ye."

' I need not trouble you with all the details of my walk, or arrival at the Hibernia; suffice it to say that neither Morton nor any message from him had come. So after leaving a few lines to be delivered to my friend immediately on his arrival, I at once prepared to make my way back to Maughold, where so much awaited me to do.

' I traversed the same road, passing Corna Bay. The morning was opening up into a bright one, that seemed to herald a fine day; the sea, as far as eye could reach, looked like a spread of glittering silver in the gleams of early sunrise. I neared the cottage where Cecil had told me the McInnises lived: smoke was curling up from the solitary chimney. They had risen, then. I would make inquiries of the man whom Morton had said he would get to row him to Ramsey. How had not this occurred to me before? He, perhaps, would be able to tell me of my friend—might even have been charged with a message that he had failed to deliver.

' As I was threading my way along the shingly beach, a man came out of the hut. He carried what seemed a heavily-laden sack upon his shoulders, and made his way with difficulty (half staggering under the load) towards a boat that I saw in the distance, gently rising and falling on the shining water with every

movement of the tide.   This no doubt would be
McInnis.

' " Hie—I say !" I shouted; but he either did not
or would not hear—the latter I concluded, for he
presently quickened his pace, and I saw for the first
time that he limped badly.   Of whom did he remind
me ?   My dream !   I now ran rapidly after him—he
heard me ; and, turning for one second, and seeing I
was pursuing, still further increased his speed.   That
momentary glimpse of his face showed me the
counterpart of the murderer of my vision !—nightmare !—call it what you will.   Good God !   Then
had all the horrors I had witnessed when in that
mesmeric state been a true warning or prophecy of
what had now been fulfilled ?   A cold moisture broke
out over my head, yet still I ran after the man ; and he,
perceiving I was swiftly gaining on him, put the sack
down on the beach, and seated himself on it, as
though awaiting me.

' " Sure an' are ye wanting me, sorr ?" he asked, as I
arrived panting at his side.

' " Yes, I am wanting you," I replied angrily;
"and why did you not stop when I shouted to
you ?"

' " I did not hear, your honour, or av coorse I'd
have waited ; I'm rayther hard of hearin'.   And what
might yer be wanting wid me, sorr ?"

' " You are named McInnis, are you not ?"

' " Yis, sorr ; Pat McInnis at yer honour's sarvice."

'"Well, now, Pat McInnis, I happen to know that my friend Mr. Cecil Morton went out with you yesterday in your boat. He has not returned home, so I come to you for information about him."

'And I looked steadily and sternly at him. He moved his shifty eyes uneasily for a moment under my searching gaze, but soon recovered himself.

'"So yer honour's a frind of the dear young gintleman's?" he said, wiping his mouth on the back of his grimy-looking hand; "an' it's proud I am to hear that same, for it's meself didn't know what to do about him at all, at all. He didn't go in the boat yestherday, yer honour, but he came for me, sorr, and I wint wid him to the rocks beyant, and his fut slipt, and his head is hurted—badly, I'm thinking; for he's not spaking nor moving, and what he does say there isn't no sinse in; and it's meself is just going in the boat to get a docther from town to come to see him— indade, the quicker I go the betther. Maybe yer honour would not be above helping me wid this sack to the little craft, for I'se got to fetch it; an' then, sorr, if yer'll go back to that cottage there, you'll find Misthriss McInnis and the young gintleman."

'Then Cecil was alive! and, bad as the news was as to his state, how relieved I felt! I gladly helped the man with his load. He rowed briskly away, and presently disappeared round the nearest headland. I turned with a lightened heart to the little thatched cabin, and knocked at the door, but no one answered,

nor did I hear any sound to indicate that it was in-
habited.   What was the meaning of this?   I tried the
latch, but found that entrance was barred from within.
There was a place for a window, but innocent of frame
or glass ; in their stead was a strong wooden shutter.
On trying this, I found it also was securely fastened
inside !   My fears revived with redoubled force.   The
man's tale, could it have been concocted on the
instant, to send me back, and gain time to effect his
escape?   Alas ! I feared so.

'"Mrs. McInnis ! Mrs. McInnis !"   I   shouted,
rattling the latch furiously at the same time.

'No answer ; but as I listened, I could distinguish
cautious movements inside.

'" I implore you, tell me," I cried, "whoever you
may be, is there a gentleman in this hut, who has been
badly hurt by a fall from the rocks ?"

'"No, no, no !" wailed a female voice ; and then a
low moan fell upon my ear.   "Go away ! go away !
for the love of heaven !"

'"I will not go away, so open the door, or I will
break it down ;" and I threw myself frantically against
it ; the wood cracked in places, I could hear, but did
not otherwise yield to my desperate onslaught.
"Very well, then, unless you at once admit me, I will
make my way to the police station, and have you
and your husband arrested, and that without delay."

'Again a faint movement inside, and then I heard

the bolts being hesitatingly and slowly withdrawn ; the door opened, and there stood *the woman of my vision* —tall and thin, and clad in long, black, clinging garments, the same dark, crape-like covering enveloping her head. A chill of dread and fear crept over me. For a few seconds I could not speak, but gazed in astonishment at the strange figure.

' " Is there a gentleman concealed in this cottage, badly injured from a fall ?" I tremblingly asked.

' " No, no, no," again wailed the woman ; " go away ! go away !"

' " Not till I have searched every hole and corner of this place. Stand out of the way, and let me pass ;" for she had tried to bar my entrance.

' I put her to one side, and as I crossed the threshold she glided past me, wringing her hands like the dream-woman, and moved swiftly away in the direction of the beach. I did not wait to detain her, but took a hasty survey of the hut ; but, save a tail-less red cat that sprang from the hearth on to a large sea-chest near, from whence it growled and spit at me, no other living thing was in the place.

' I had been tricked, deceived, and had actually helped the murderer, as I now believed him to be, to escape—the thief—with what he had stolen from his victim. I was now fully persuaded that all I had witnessed a week before was a marvellous premonition, or " warning." I had for the time been vested with the power of " second-sight ;" perhaps the

"gift," as some call it, was latent in me. I had
suffered myself to be laughed out of all faith in the
revelation. For this I should suffer a life-long repent-
ance. Grief, every other thought or feeling, was now
in abeyance to the one burning desire for vengeance.
He who had done this deed should not escape me.
Full of this idea, and dreading that the villain might
escape, I made all haste to Ramsey, not even pausing
to enter the cottage where my dear grandmother lay.
I ran rather than walked—my blood was in a fever ;
but why should I trouble you with the feelings of that
time? I must confine myself to the bare details, and
these I shall give as succinctly as possible.

'I went at once to the police-station on arriving in
the town. I need hardly say I did not subject myself
to ridicule by relating what I have told you. All that
could be done was done, and with wonderful expedi-
tion, notwithstanding the slowness with which the
Manx police force are sometimes charged ; but neither
the man nor woman McInnis, or any trace of them,
could be found.

'The next thing I did was to write to Mr. Haynes,
telling him of Morton's mysterious disappearance, my
encounter with the McInnises, and stating also that I
had every reason to fear there had been foul play on
the part of the Irishman. This Mr. Haynes was
married to Morton's sister. She was your uncle's
favourite of the few remaining to him of his relatives.
By the way, is she alive now?'

Mr. Parker paused to inquire. Having informed him that she and her husband had years ago joined the great majority, he proceeded :

'My next movement was to remove all my belongings from the inn to Mrs. Quayle's cottage at Maughold, where my dear grandmother had spent so many years of her life.

' Mr. Haynes arrived the day after I had followed my much-loved relative to her last resting-place. He had started immediately on receipt of my letter. He was, as, of course, you are aware, a solicitor, a self-possessed, business-like man, who questioned me very calmly, and without any display of emotion, as to all the particulars of his brother-in-law's disappearance, his general habits, and so on. He considered what I related of the Irishman very damning evidence against him, and, like myself, was inclined to believe the worst. Before driving out to me, he had, he told me. ordered posters, offering a reward of £100 for any information respecting Morton. He returned that evening to Ramsey, where he had put up at the —— Hotel.

'Thoroughly weary, I retired early to bed, and soon forgot everything in the sound sleep of exhaustion. Towards six o'clock next morning, I was roused by loud knocking at my door. In answer to a rather drowsy "Come in," Mrs. Quayle called to me in frightened tones :

' "Oh, sir ! please get up ; yer wanted."

'I jumped out of bed at once.

'"What is it?" I cried.

'"Loss-a-me, I don't know rightly how to tell ye, an' that's the thruth; but, sir, the poor young gentleman, he's—he's——"

'All this time I had been hastily donning my garments.

'"He's what?" and I opened the door.

'"He's found——"

'"He's found, thank God!"

'"Oh, but he's——"

'"Where—where? Speak, can't you?" for the terrified woman seemed hardly able to utter a word. "Oh, tell me, Mrs. Quayle; pray collect yourself. He is lying badly injured somewhere, perhaps."

'I asked this, though from the poor landlady's agitated appearance I anticipated what she found so difficult to say.

'"Injured! The Lord be good to us! No, no, sir; but dead he is. Picked up, the corpse was, by Jemmy Kinraid and Charley Fell this mornin'. They were goin' out early to the fishin', an' some boy with them, an' they seen something floating; an' when they come near, they seen it was a body, and they took it into the boat—a terrible sight, they're sayin'. But they foun' out who he was with letters an' writin' in his pockets; an' then they took the poor lad to the Hibernia, an' they wasn' willin' there for to take him in. But there he is, anyways, poor young falla!

Och, och! an' sorry enough I am that the like should happen to him."

'My distress, all the painful after-details, I spare you, and at once turn to the time, five years later, when I again visited the Isle of Man. I pass over the intervening visits, as they were quite uneventful. I was now a married man, and doing very well in the business in which I and my son are now partners; but I had never forgotten my friend Cecil Morton, or ceased to think, with deep pain, of his tragic end, nor had years weakened my faith in my having had revealed by second-sight how this dreadful tragedy had been brought about. I always put up at Mrs. Quayle's in Maughold, and each time inquired whether anything had been heard of the McInnises. They had totally disappeared—had not even tried to reclaim their goods and chattels at the cottage. An elderly woman of the name of Kneale, who, I was informed, was aunt to Mrs. McInnis, went in, and took possession; and as she paid the owner of the little place the trifling rent regularly, she stayed there unopposed. The time of my visit to the island of which I am about to speak was in the beginning of October. The weather was anything but pleasant— gusty and cold, with occasional heavy downpours of rain. The sky kept up a dull, leaden-gray appearance, through which the sun shed only watery beams; whilst the sea came rolling in, in huge, dark, threaten- ing waves, crested here and there with white foam

that either broke with sullen roar upon the beach, or
dashed with impotent fury against the rocky coast
that impeded its progress.

'The third day after my arrival at Mrs. Quayle's a
storm of unusual severity set in. The wind howled
and shrieked round the little cottage, shaking it to the
foundations, as though bent upon its destruction. A
threatening gloom hung over the whole landscape,
while the loud boom of the sea sounded out in
sonorous tone above the raging wind and beating rain.
This tempest continued with unabated violence
throughout the night, but towards morning began to
moderate, and by eight o'clock the sun broke through,
and at last dispersed the overhanging clouds. A faint
breeze only stirred the air, or shook the glistening
raindrops from the laden trees. No trace of the
previous night's hurricane remained, save the wet
ground and deep pools that overflowed, sending tiny
rivulets down hedges and paths in all directions.

'"There was a wreck off Maughold Head las'
night, sir," said my landlady as she was removing my
breakfast things.

'"Indeed ! No lives lost, I hope ?"

'"I can't say for sure, but one man, I hear, got
ashore—jus' by yonther steep rocks by Corna Bay ;
an' it's a wonder if he got up so far as he was tellin',
for he was jus' at the top, when down he fell to the
bottom ; an' his back is broke, an' Docther Christian
says there isn' no hopes of him. He was took to

Misthress Kneale's cottage by them as foun' him, it bein' the neares'. Quayle has gone over now to see how is he. He's talkin'—the man, I mean, that's hurted—of two others as was wis him in the smack. They, it seems, were left on her, but he was swep' off by a heavy sea that washed her decks."

' " I'll go and see if I can do anything for the poor fellow ;" and I at once started for the cottage where the unfortunate man lay.

'Some half dozen people were congregated near the door, talking, who touched their hats civilly to me as I passed into the hut.

' " He's been ramblin' a bit, sir," said Mrs. Kneale, " an' mus' be kep' quite (quiet). He's not to see no one ;" and she tried to bar my further progress towards the bed by placing her broad rotund figure between me and it in an almost threatening attitude that surprised me.

'I was about to retire quietly, when, by a sudden restless movement of his arm, the man threw down a curtain that had hung from the ceiling, and before the bed, and had completely concealed it and him from my view ; but now he lay clearly revealed before me —*no other than McInnis !*

' Mrs. Kneale picked up and tried hastily to replace the fallen drapery, but before she could interfere I pushed past her to the side of the bed.

' " Is that a priest ?" asked the man. "Oh, for the love of Heaven, get me a priest ! Oh ! the saints be

4

good to me ! What did all the goold, and the watch,
and the things—what did they bring me?" he moaned:
"nothing but ill luck, and misfortin', and mortial fear
night and day—night and day ! And he niver
doubtin' but going wid me, the craythur—and me to
strike him down like that ! What divil put yonder bit
of leaded stick into my hand? Blissid Virgin, pray
for me ! Jesus, pray for me ! Oh, that I could
remimber the words good Father Hamilton used to
tache me! It was the just judgment of God upon me
—that I should be kilt—aff av the same rocks as I
sint—him ! Oh, will I be ha'nted for iver and always
—with him falling—falling——"

'"Come away, sir — ye'd betther," said Mrs.
Kneale, taking hold of my arm ; "it's ravin' the poor
falla is."

'"It is McInnis, and you know it;" and I shook
myself free of her. "He is now beyond the reach of
human justice, so you need be in no fear at my recog-
nising him, or of anyone else ; but is there no priest
to be got for the poor creature?" for the dying man
was again petitioning imploringly in the midst of his
delirium for "a priest—a priest."

'"Pries'," said Mrs. Kneale contemptuously ; "what
good would the like do him, or anyone else? I've sent
for a neighbour man. He's a local preacher, too, an'
he'll put up a bit of a prayer with him. I'm pityin'
him enough, poor sowl, though he was a rale bad man
to my niece—his wife, she was. She was drove out of

her right sinses with him, an' that fond of him, too, for all, that she'd be followin' him about everywhere, for fear he'd be took for smugglin', or some of his bad doin's—watchin' him—watchin' him—still she was; an' she could climb up—up an' down the highest places, and the roughest, like a goat. She took a quare notion to wear a long black dhress, an' she was puttin' a wisp of crape on her head—down to her knees nearly—when she'd be goin' out, instead of a decent bonnet. I'm wondtherin' where'll she be now."

' "A priest!—a priest!" again moaned the wretched man.

' Presently his mood changed; he tried to raise himself in the bed, shrieking in agonized tones: " Take him away! I'm seeing him always and iver, with the look—he turned on me when he was falling—falling." His voice then sank to a low murmur. " Hide it— hide it, wife. Ned Dougherty and me—in the fishing lugger—*Gipsy Queen*. I rowed out—Ned was drunk. I waited till night—threw the body overboard. Wake up, Ned—we must get under way—for Whitehaven. Ned mustn't know the goold I've got hid away in the *Gipsy Queen*—and in the cave off Maughold Head. No one knows that cave but you—and me—Janie!"

' "Could you not find out from him before he becomes quite unconscious what has become of his unfortunate wife?" I said to Mrs. Kneale.

' "I've been thryin', but I'll thry him agen;" and she bent over McInnis, putting her mouth close

4—2

to his ear, asked slowly and clearly: "Where's Janie?"

' He turned his dazed eyes apprehensively upon her for a moment.

'"Janie?—yis, sure—where is she? Poor Janie!" he muttered, moving his head restlessly backwards and forwards upon the pillow, as if endeavouring to recall something. "Why, Janie, yer not going to die and lave me all alone?" and his voice became wonderfully soft and gentle. He was evidently in imagination living over again the scene of his wife's death— their parting. "I've not been what I ought to ye, asthore, but you were the good faithful woman to me, and ivery crass word and ivery blow that I gave you I'm regritting now. Sorrow a wan will ye git from Pat agin if ye'll git betther. What's that yer saying, mavourneen. Spake up! Ye can't? Ah, well, don't throuble. I'm clear now in my head. 'Pat, dear' (yis, that's what she's saying), 'my brain was clouded for long, but I've loved you through all, Pat, an' am only thinkin' of what a good man ye wor to me—afore you got into bad company; an' now—now I'm leaving ye, promise me ye'll thry to lead a betther life.' An' is that what yer sayin', asthore. Arrah, but I've that on my sowl that'll niver be forgotten night nor day— waking nor slaping! Go on my knees and pray—me is it? Who'd listen to me? He that died for me and all the wurrold—'ready to pardon and recave the pinitent sinner.' An' sure, mavourneen, how could the likes of me git to Him widout the priest; but I'll go to his riverence and—oh, Janie!—mavourneen!—wife!—it's not dead ye are—ay, dead—*dead!*—poor girl!—buried—far away—in America—where *his* money—took us—Janie. Send for Father Hamilton —quick!—quick!" again he cried in agonized tones.

'Just then the doctor came in, accompanied—as his dress proclaimed him—by a priest, and I at once withdrew.

'Did I want further confirmation of the truth of the vision? What fills me with undying regret is, that I had been laughed out of heeding and acting on the warning given me by second-sight.'

And so ended this strange history. I had been much struck with Mr. Parker's clear recollection, not only of all the incidents, but of even the words spoken so many years past, and also that he seemed to fall naturally—when relating dialogue—from his very pure English to the vernacular of the Manx or Irish, as the case might be.

The acquaintanceship I had made in the little way-side inn with father and son ripened into a warm friendship. The old man has now for years been gathered to his rest, and his grand-daughter, the child of 'Masther George,' is now my wife.

Mrs. Rachel Looney—the eccentric landlady—I heard, had not long after undertaken the journey to Adelaide, there to remain with some relatives. She had been enriched, report said, by the discovery of some valuable coins on her property at Ballabarna, in Maughold. These coins, I was also informed, she sent out of the island—lest they might be claimed and sold in England—with the exception of four. These a Mr. Wallace, of Dissington, near White-haven, who happened to be in the island about that time, bought from a jeweller in Douglas. Only two of the four could be deciphered—both Anglo-Saxon— one a Sihtric, the other an Ethelred. This was about the year 1834. But many people now living remember the strange landlady of the Hibernia, though the sad tragedy is forgotten that occurred off Maughold Head.

THE LEGEND OF ST. MICHAEL'S ISLE.

THE LEGEND OF ST. MICHAEL'S ISLE.

Father Kelly and his little charge—The priest's wondrous vision
—The chapel of Keeihl Vaayle—Paul and Ayla—The war
arrow—Battle in Ramsey Bay—Paul rescues Dugal—Discovery of Ayla by her parents—The priest's strange adventure in the chapel—Ayla's and Paul's marriage at Keeihl
Vaayle—Murder of the good Father—Death of the murderer
—Conclusion.

AT the southern extremity of the Isle of Man is a
place called Langness, a sort of peninsula, to which is
attached the diminutive island of St. Michael's, in
the present day known as Fort Island.

At the time of which we write, somewhere about
the middle of the eleventh century, during the reign
of Godred II. in Man, and when the insular Church
was governed by good Bishop Gamaliel, a strange
group were gathered on this isle. Old men leaning
heavily on their staves, or supported by their strong,
stalwart-looking sons or grandsons, women, too, of
all ages, swelled the number, while little children
either played at hide-and-seek with each other—much
the same as the young people of the present day—or
sat here and there gathering the flowers of both land
and sea growth, that so plentifully besprinkled the

short green sward, while those of more tender years
were carried in their mothers' arms. All bent their
eyes anxiously on the remarkable figure approaching
them—an aged priest, whose cowl now covered his
head. He led by the hand a little child of perhaps
six or seven years old, and as he drew nearer, the
people, one and all, bowed in reverence, and then
bent their eyes inquiringly on their pastor. Before
addressing them he ascended a sort of cairn, or heap
of stones, that were piled together near, thus raising
himself a little above the crowd, and throwing back
his hood, displayed a face on which relentless time
had traced many a wrinkle; but years had not dimmed
the fire of the deep-set black eyes, shaded by thick
gray brows. The nose was aquiline, the forehead
broad, the head surrounded by a fringe of snow-white
hair, and now, as his gaze travelled from one to
another of those about him, a smile of infinite gentleness lighted up the whole face, softening a countenance
that in repose looked harsh and stern.

The little girl had dropped his hand at a whisper
from him, and joined a group of children near, to
whom she showed in strong contrast, not only by the
beauty and delicacy of her complexion, and the finer
cast of features and of limbs, but in her dress, which
was of rich materials, not worn or manufactured in
the island, both women and children being clad in
the warm rough sort of flannel, or cloth, spun from
the wool of the Loaghtyn sheep.

The priest, amidst a profound silence, broken only by the soft lap of the sea against the cliffs, lifted his hands, as though invoking a blessing, and then raising his eyes to heaven, his voice in solemn tones fell upon the ear of those around, as he said in Manx: 'Ayns Eunym yn Ayr, as y Vac, as y Spyrryd Noo' ('In the name of the Father, the Son and the Holy Ghost').

After a moment's pause he said : 'I have asked you all to meet me here, when the sun is not long risen, whilst his rays still kindle into light, the early dew on grass and flower, before you go this bright April morning to your daily labour. The first and the last of the day ought always to be dedicated in worship and in prayer to the God who has given it, and whose holy angels guard us, not only in the silent watches of the night, but in the busy hours of toil.'

The priest again paused before saying : 'I have matter of great import to tell you. Yesterday, about mid-day, a sudden strange sleep, or unconsciousness, fell upon me ; and methought God's holy angel, St. Michael, stood beside me. His raiment shone like the glitter of the sea where the moonbeams fall. Round his head a halo of light gleamed as a crown of glory ; the beauty of his face was such as no painting of even our Blessed Lady could picture.

'I would have fallen on my knees before him, but he stayed me, saying :

'"Do not bend the knee to me, but follow where I am bid to lead thee."

'I, trembling, rose, for such awe did fill my senses at this wondrous vision that my limbs would scarce obey my willing mind.

'"Good and faithful servant of the Most High," said he, "fear not;" and, taking my hand, methought that he and I rose softly from the earth, and floated in the air, hand in hand, till we stood where we are all assembled, on this little isle.'

Here excited murmurs from the listeners broke in upon the priest's address. Some fell on their knees, and many of the women prostrated themselves in prayer; exclamations of wonder, and even dread, rose on every side, while glances of fear and expectation were cast around. Children stopped their play, and the little ones clung to their mothers' knees.

The speaker, seeing the effect of his words, changed his tone:

'Are ye not proud, instead of fearful?' he cried, while his eyes shot fire from beneath their shaggy brows, 'that a message from heaven should be sent to you, and that the archangel himself should be the messenger? And that message was—what think ye? That *here*, on this very spot where we are all assembled —here, I say, you and I, working together, are to build a church for the service of *God;* and now I ask: Are ye all ready to do what ye can in this pious work? Money you have not, but most of you have strong hands. Have you willing hearts?'

Cries of 'The! the!' ('Yes! yes!') arose on every

side. Women wept and crossed themselves, while men clasped hands, and all vowed to do their utmost in this great work. The priest, after a few more words of exhortation and prayer, dismissed them ; and as they made their way back to their respective homes, they talked, in awe-struck tones, of the wonderful vision of the good father.

'I bless God and His saints,' said one old graybeard, 'that I have been spared to see the day when an angel from heaven should be sent to us. I mind the time when good Father Kelly came from Ireland. We were little better than heathen, though we had heard of Christ and His Gospel ; but he has worked among us early and late. Where sickness or sorrow comes, there he is always found, helping and comforting ; and many a day and many a night has he passed in fast and vigil, praying for our souls. How good must he be, and saintly, and beloved, when the holy angel St. Michael has been sent to him ! Isn't it wonderful—wonderful? These hands are old and feeble, but methinks I can carry a few stones to the work ; but help I must, and help I will !'

His words were taken up by all within hearing, and 'Help we must, and help we will !' was echoed in the Manx tongue on all sides by the excited crowd.

And now ten years have passed, and the little chapel of Keeihll Vaayl (St. Michael's) stands as complete, and has done for some six years, as rough hands could make it. The people had never flagged in their energy, even after the excitement of the good priest's address had to a certain extent worn off; they had devoted every hour to the work that they could spare from toiling on their farms, or out at the fishing, to provide for the wants of their families and themselves.

Cummings, in his ' Isle of Man,' thus describes the ruins of this chapel still to be seen on St. Michael's or Fort Island :

'The little Isle of St. Michael (commonly called Fort Island), on which stands the fort and ruined church, is connected with Langness at its northern point by a narrow causeway. . . .

' There can be no doubt of the great antiquity of the little chapel, or oratory, at the west end of it. Two centuries ago, as figured in Chaloner's " Description," it was a ruin. It reminds us strongly in its architecture and general details of the interesting church of Peransabuloe in Cornwall. It differs, however, in the number of windows. The church of Peransabuloe was lighted by but *one*, this has *four*, an east and a west window, and a north and south placed very near the east end. The west, north, and south windows are square-headed, the two latter being only twelve inches wide outside, but with a wide splay to two feet ten inches inside. The east window is one long single light, with a semicircular head and only ten inches in breadth outside, but largely splayed.

' This little chapel is of but one compartment,

whose length is thirty-one feet, and breadth fourteen. The thickness of the walls is three feet. At the west end is a bell-turret. The chapel was entered by one door on the south side, nine feet from the west end, the height of which is six feet, and the width two feet four inches. This door, like the east window, has a semicircular heading, formed of small pieces of the schist of this neighbourhood, set edgeways round the arch, whilst the door-jambs are of rough blocks of lime-stone. There is no appearance of a tool on any part of it, if we except the coping stones on the west gable.

'We may mark the foundation of a stone altar under the east window, and at the same end, on the north corner, three stone steps which may have served as an ambo or pulpit. The height of the side-walls of the building is only ten feet. The length of its graveyard is one hundred and ninety-two feet, and the breadth ninety-eight, and as yet it is untouched by the plough.'

But to return to our story. On this particular day—a warm, bright one for the season, February—two figures might be seen resting beneath the shelter of the chapel porch. The one, a young girl of rare beauty, whose golden hair fell in silky waves below her waist; her complexion vied in colouring with the tinting of the pink-lined shell she held within the taper fingers of her small white hand; her features were exquisitely formed, while the large dark-blue eyes she now and then raised to her companion's face were lovely, not only from shape and colour, but by their earnest, trustful expression.   She was clothed in the rough woollen dress worn by the natives of the Isle of Man ; but nothing could conceal the grace of her figure, or take from a certain air of gentle birth that had earned for her the title amongst the people round of 'the priest's little lady.'

Leaning against the entrance-door of the chapel, at her side, stood her companion, a young man of about twenty years of age.   He was quite six feet high, with a strong and well-knit frame.   His eyes, hair, and eye-brows were very dark, and the first appearance of a beard showed black upon his upper lip and cheeks. His head, which he had uncovered, was well formed, the forehead broad and high, the nose straight, and the shapely mouth and chin beneath seemed to indicate firmness and stability of character.   Though he, too, is dressed in the rough costume of a Manx peasant, it is evident that he is of much higher degree, his whole air and appearance being that of one used rather to handle the sword than till the ground, to tread in courts instead of the humble abode of an island agriculturist or fisherman.

He addresses his companion in English : 'Then thou dost not remember any time before thou camest to the good father ?'

'Methinks I have some dim recollections, so faint as almost to seem like dreams, of a time when I used to see armed men go forth, as if to battle, when the sound of music and of clanking spears did break

in upon my infant slumbers, and that, when I cried at
the sound, someone beautiful as one of God's angels
did bend over me and soothe me into rest, and then
more vividly I remember being in a ship with rough,
fierce men about me : I can still picture them, and the
great waves that seemed each moment going to bury
us beneath their black waters. I recollect next
waking from sleep or unconsciousness, and instead of
the cruel-looking people who had surrounded and
terrified me, and the sea, and the rocking of the ship,
I was being gently carried in the priest's arms. I have
only confused memories. This is all—and it seems
hardly real.'

'And what has the good father told you? Where
did he find you, dear one?'

'Wrapped in warm furs in the shelter of the
cliffs near. At first he thought me dead; but as he
bent o'er me, mine eyes unclosed, and gazed,' he
said, 'in such fear and wonder in his face as made
him sad to see. He took me in his arms, and brought
me to his home, where he and his good sister cared
for and tended me ever since with such gentleness
and affection I can ne'er repay, save by the devoted love I bear them. Mistress Kelly, his sister,
told me they asked whence I came, and all I could
reply was "big ship," "black water," and "bad men,"
and that my name was Ayla, and at times, at first,
I cried, and could scarce be comforted, to be taken
to my mother and Olave, and sometimes from my

5

indistinct speech they thought they could gather
names like Angus and Dugall.   Slipped between
the clothes on me, they found this.'

And Ayla drew from her bosom a massive gold
chain, to which was attached a cross of the same
metal ; on the back of this were rudely traced some
letters and the representation of a battle-axe of the
period.   The young man looked carefully at this for
some time, and while he was examining it, the girl
continued :

'Within the furs in which I was enveloped were
some articles of rich clothing, and the good father and
Mistress Kelly wished to lay these things by ; but
when they went to dress me in this woollen stuff that
I wear now, I cried and fretted so they let me have
my will, and I wore the things they found with me till
I grew too big for them ; and they have kept them torn
and worn as they are, thinking that by them, and this
piece of ornament you hold, those to whom I belonged,
if they sought me, might know me for their child.'

Ayla paused, and looked dreamily out to where the
sea lay calm and blue beyond :

'I have had dreams and fancies that the beautiful
lady I seem to remember might some day come across
those waters, and, landing, find me here.   Ofttimes I
have fallen asleep thinking how happy I should be to
feel her arms fold round me, and that I should call her
"mother"—idle dreams ! And I have been left naught
I ought to desire.   Kindness and even lavish affection

have been bestowed upon me by both Mistress Kelly
and the good father, and all the people round love me,
and I them.'

'And now thou hast my devoted love, my Ayla,
and yet, alas ! I scarce know how to tell thee, but I
must bid thee farewell !'

'What, dost thou leave thine Ayla ?' she cried, in
startled accents.

'"Tis even so, beloved ! the war-arrow summons
me, like many others, to the fight.'

'To fight !' echoed Ayla, in frightened tones ; 'oh,
Paul, my beloved—my dearest, I cannot let thee go !
I cannot part from thee !' In an agony of grief
she threw her arms around her lover and held him,
as though by this means she could keep him by her
side.

'Go I must, my loved one, and my heart is torn
with anguish that I must part with thee. But two
moons have come and gone since, idly wandering here
after visiting the good monks at Rushen, I saw thee
in that bay gathering shells. How beautiful thou
wert ! I loved thee then, and ever shall. Alas that I
should have to leave thee, my sweet Ayla !' he
murmured tenderly, as he held her in his arms.
'Thou hast perchance heard that a conspiracy is set
on foot by Torfinn, son of Ottar, against the good
King Godred to depose him from this, his kingdom of
Man. In this Torfinn is helped by Somerled, Moarmor of Argyle ; and to warn Godred, my father, Paul

Balkason, Lord of Skye, came hither, bringing me
with him ; and so, as I told thee, dear one, the war-
arrow hath been despatched ordering the preparation
of ships, and to-morrow, ere the sun shows above yon
waters, we shall have sailed from hence to meet the
enemy.   I fear me that I cared not much for listening to my father and your king, or those that advised
with them, discussing all the preparations for this war,
though my blood warms and my heart beats high at
the thought of the coming battle.'

‘ Ah, how different art thou then to me,’ sighed Ayla ;
‘ my blood runs cold, and my heart sinks low in
dread at what may befall thee in the fight ! If thou art
slain, I can but lay me down and die, for live without thee now I cannot.’

‘ My loved one, my Ayla !’ cried Paul, as he
kissed the tear-stained face, ‘ thou shouldest be brave,
and think only of the time when I shall return and in
this very church make thee my wife, to love thee ever,
and cherish thee, and keep thee by my side.’

‘ And here,’ said Ayla, ‘ will I repair each day to
pray for thee ! May God, and our Lady, and the good
St. Michael guard thee, and bring thee safe back to
thine Ayla ;’ and the girl devoutly crossed herself,
her lover following her example.

And now in vows of love, passionate kisses, and
sighs, with many tears the lovers try to part, and once
and again, and yet again, they take what is to be the
last embrace, and yet Paul cannot tear himself away,

until the lengthening shadows warn Ayla that she has been long from home, that Mistress Kelly will be uneasy, and perhaps angered ; and besides this, threatening clouds are rising above the horizon far out to sea, and she remembers Paul has many miles to walk before he can get to Duglas, where he stays that night, and joins his father and the king, and next morning all take ship to meet Prince Somerled, who is advancing, it is said, with a fleet of eighty galleys to meet the opposing forces of the King of Man.

When Ayla got home, she found Mistress Kelly as she feared, uneasy at her lengthened absence, and not a little put about that her brother, who had gone to shrive a dying man in a hamlet some miles distant, had not yet returned, as she, too, had marked the signs of a coming storm, and feared his being wet and roughly handled by the rising wind.

She had piled turf and large logs of wood on the wide hearth, and as Ayla warmed herself she, for the first time, noticed how pale and sad, and what a tear-stained face the firelight revealed.

' My little lady,' she cried, ceasing from the lecture she had been administering on the impropriety of wandering for hours by the sea instead of being employed in some useful way, or studying some of the many things the priest had given her to learn— ' why, little lady, what ails thee? art thou ill? or has aught happened to distress thee ?'

And for all answer Ayla threw her arms round the

good woman's neck, and wept and sobbed, and at last
in broken phrases told her all her sorrow : how Paul—
to whom Mistress Kelly was well affected—would sail
with the ships to-morrow, and perhaps be killed, and
never return to gladden her with his presence again.
'Then, indeed,' she moaned, ' would the sky look ever
black, and even the summer breeze seem to echo
sighs, whilst flowers would lose their beauty and their
scent ; the murmur of the sea and the song of the
birds would have for me but one sad sound — death,
death !'

'Why, Ayla, Ayla, this is very wrong ! such worship should be given to none on earth.   God gives us
friends to love, and to be loved by, and duties to
fulfil for them, and all about us ; these things are to
lighten what would, perchance, otherwise be an over-
toilsome road to heaven ; we are to help each other
on the way ; but God should be first of all in our
thoughts and heart, and all His gifts we should be
ready to resign at His most sacred will.'

'I could never be ready to resign my love, or say
" God's will be done " to that ; perchance, if I live to
be so old as thou art, I may feel like thee.'

'Hoot, tut ! prithee rouse thee ; thy Paul will come
back safe enough, never fear thee,' cried Mistress
Kelly testily, not too well pleased at this allusion
to her years ; 'and thou wilt be his wife, thou'lt see,
and have enough of him, and he of thee, maybe ; there's
naught that cools the frenzy of love like years of

wedded life and constant intercourse, I am told by those who've put it to the test. Holy Father!' she exclaimed in a changed voice, as a gust of wind swept past the house, seeming to shake it to the very foundation, 'list to the storm, how it rises, and see the heavens, how black they have become! I fear me thy Paul and Brian will have a wet skin ere they get to shelter; Paul, being young and strong, will suffer no more than the discomfort; but for my brother, who hath numbered eighty years, I fear it may go hard! I trust he will remain the night where he hath gone, and not attempt to brave the coming storm.'

Her uneasiness communicated itself to Ayla, who looked forth; and certainly the scene was enough to cause both women great anxiety. The sea that had had almost a summer aspect a few hours before, reflected now the blackness of the threatening clouds overhead, the rumble of distant thunder broke upon the ear, and presently a blinding flash of lightning gleamed across the bay, followed by a roar of thunder so terrific that both the frightened women involuntarily clasped hands in sympathetic terror, whilst the serving-woman rushed in from the kitchen exclaiming in frightened accents and the Manx tongue:

'God be good to us! but is not this terrible—*terrible!* I'm trembling, not for the storm, though I've ne'er seen nor heard the like before; but the good father, where will he be now? God and His holy angels have him in their keeping!'

Meanwhile, the priest had long before started on his homeward way; he, nor those whom he had left, had not observed—they in their grief, and he in his perfect sympathy—the lowering sky nor rising wind. Armed with a stout staff, he trudged along with a strength and activity wonderful for his years.

'Ah me!' he murmured, 'how oft have I trod these paths to shrive the dying, to minister to the sick, to comfort those in sorrow, to help the poor in so far as I could compass, and, what seemeth to me whereof more to rejoice, to lead the thoughts and desires of all from earth to heaven! And I have hereof much wherein to glory, in that God hath blessed mine efforts, and many have been led to the faithful worship of Him. Should not this content me? Alas, it doth not! May He forgive me, for methinks I cannot die content till I see the Chapel of St. Michael with an altar, such as has gladdened mine eyes in many a church in mine own land—ay, or such an one as at the abbey at Russin. It did not seem an idle dream to trust, as so ofttimes I have done, that when St. Michael himself did vouchsafe to appear to me and bid me raise this chapel to his honour, that so wonderful a vision might be followed by miraculous guidance and assistance to furnish the interior with all it now lacks. Yet all these years have passed, and I fear me that to others will be left the task to finish that which I began;' and the good old man sighed heavily; the patience and resignation he preached to others he found it hard to exercise in this the great desire of his simple earnest life.

' I will e'en now hie me to the church, and pass the few hours of the remaining day in prayer " for help, for guidance, for *submission*." '

He had still some little way to go, and had barely gained the entrance to the chapel when the threatened storm burst forth in all its fury. He made haste to get within the shelter of the church, and groped his way where some flickering lights shed the feeble rays that helped to guide him to the altar, where he devoutly knelt.

This altar was a simple slab of stone supported on pillars and marked with five crosses cut on the top, signifying the five wounds of our Lord. By the decree of the Council of Epone in France, A.D. 509, ' no altars were to be consecrated with the chrism of holy oil, but such as were made of stone only.'

Unmindful of the fearful uproar, the lightning that every now and then illumined the place, the thunder, or the tempest that beat upon the sacred edifice, and seemed each moment to threaten its destruction, the good old man prayed on, calm and undisquieted. Erelong the wind abated, and at last died down, sobbing itself into quietness like a tired child; the peals of thunder and flashes of lightning came at greater intervals; and for the first time it dawned upon Father Kelly's mind that his sister and Ayla would probably be in great anxiety as to his safety. He rose from his knees, intending to make his way to where he could look out upon the night, and so judge as to when it might be possible to get to his home, but was arrested by the sound of hasty stumbling footsteps and men's voices speaking low and hurriedly.

Presently the steps came round the chapel, paused by the entrance; the door was tried, and after a little delay opened. The priest made haste to ascend the few steps that led to the ambo or pulpit, where in the semi-darkness he hoped to find a place of secure concealment. The men, with uncertain tread, as though carrying some heavy weight, came in, and with many oaths dropped their burden on the floor.

'Beshrew thee for a careless fool, Niel!' cried one. 'Where in the name of the —— can this be hidden, and in a chapel too, by all that is holy? I like it not.'

'And beshrew thee for a doited fool!' cried the one called Niel in angry tones; ''tis thyself alone thou hast to thank that we are in this sorry plight; but hidden this must be. Go get thee one of those pale lights over there; 'twill not be a very heavy task, methinks, to raise one of these rough stones and safely hide what thou, as well as I, *know* must be hidden. Go, craven! What are ye lingering for?'

'Dost thou hear no sound?' asked the other trembling tones.

'Naught but the dying wind and the beating of your coward heart! Go, fetch the light, and with

what speed ye. may! we must haste back, and bear
us away from present pursuit.'

As the man was feeling his way slowly and carefully to do Niel's bidding, a dreadful sickening sug-
gestion as to what they were so anxious to conceal
made poor Father Kelly tremble with horror; beads
of cold perspiration gathered on his brow; a sudden
faintness seized him, and ere the altar had been
reached by the 'murderer'—as in his fear he named
him—the priest became unconscious. How long he
had remained in this state he could not tell, for when
he revived the men had gone; the first chill light of
an early morn in February was here and there making
its way into the chapel. All was still. Could he
have had some dreadful dream? and the men, their
work, their talk—could this be merely a creation of
his own excited brain? He raised his stiffened limbs
with difficulty from their cramped position, and prepared to walk as quickly home as they could bear
him. He was feeble from cold, the previous day's
fatigue, and long fast, and had neither strength nor
courage to explore the chapel or see if there was
aught to prove whether all had been only fancy, or—
and he devoutly crossed himself—a dread reality.
He reached the door in safety, and had made his way
a few steps forward, feeling a good deal revived by the
fresh morning breeze, when something glittering on
the greensward arrested his attention, and, stooping,
to his horror he beheld a dagger *stained with blood!*

He hurled the thing far from him towards the rocks beyond.

He no longer doubted that some foul deed had been done; the faintness that had before attacked him seemed to threaten him again. With steps still trembling and feeble, he hurried on, and as he neared the little thatched cottage that he called his home, he saw that he was anxiously watched for by his sister, Ayla and the serving-woman. Presently, like sounds at a distance, he knew the women were plying him with questions, to none of which he had either the strength or the desire to reply, whilst they at the same time ministered to his wants, and piled the turf on the fire in the wide hearth.

'He hath not broken bread, it's like, since yester-day at noon,' he heard the servant say; ''tis just his way to forget when he hath last fed.'

'Thou art right, good Chrissie; not since then till now have I broke my fast; but leave me to rest and in quiet for a little—my brain seems all dis-traught.'

Day wore away, and the evening shadows began to lengthen ere Father Kelly could rouse himself from the sort of half-stupor in which he had lain for hours, taking obediently, however, from time to time the nourishment the anxious women brought to his bed-side. At last a natural quiet sleep fell upon him, and in the morning he awaked refreshed, and feeling but little the effects of the fatigue, fasting, and exposure of the previous day and night. The remembrance, strange to say, of the scene in the chapel did not at first, or for many minutes, come into his mind; and when it did he knelt, as in all times of difficulty or trial good Christians ought to do, and in many prayers asked guidance from above. He could now think it all out more calmly, but before he had quite decided what his first movement ought to be, his attention was called off by hearing his sister angrily and imperatively refusing admittance to some man who was evidently equally determined to see him.

'I tell thee, Evan, 'tis not to be thought of. We feared last night he would ne'er see the morn; but, praised be the saints! a healthful sleep hath come to him, and if he be not disturbed we look to see him as well as he hath for some while been.'

The man was still pleading when, to Mistress Kelly's dismay, her brother appeared, and at once silenced her by assuming a stern, authoritative tone that no one could withstand when he saw fit to use it. When he learned that Evan bore a message from one at the point of death, and 'who prayed his ghostly help,' he at once took his staff, and, with the aid of the messenger's arm, started on his errand of mercy, leaving his poor sister muttering tearful remonstrances —she feared to speak aloud.

'"Tis but a short way, after all, and his step is wondrous strong and firm,' she said to Ayla, who had joined her at the door, and both watched the receding figures of the priest and his conductor as they made their way towards the cottage where lay the dying man.

'What aileth him?' asked Ayla ; 'and who is he?'

'None that we know. He hath lain all night at the foot of some rocks, where Evan Collett and his father found him and bore him home. He hath suffered so badly from the fall—besides, I bethink me, the young man said also from a wound—that recover he cannot, and now he lies in great pain of body, and what, alas! is worse, of soul. His name he gives as Niel. I know naught else !'

An hour or more had passed ere Father Kelly returned, and the women, who had been anxiously watching for him, were almost startled at the extraordinary change in his appearance. He left them a feeble, bent old man, requiring the aid not only of his trusty staff, but the support of the arm of the peasant who accompanied him. With tired eyes and wearied looks he went his way, and now he stood before them no longer bent and worn, but firm and erect; the eyelids were raised, showing eyes no longer weary, but bright with a light that had not shone in them for years—his whole aspect showing an energy and purpose, a look of revived hope, of an awakened interest in life, that amazed and, at the same time, perplexed his sister and Ayla, who wonderingly regarded him.

He walked restlessly up and down, seeming scarce conscious of their presence.

'Hath aught happened?' at last timidly inquired

Mistress Kelly. 'The injured man—how is he? Hath he passed away?'

'Ay,' replied the priest, ''tis even so—and in earnest contrition and true penitence for past sins. But I pray thee, good sister, question me not, but prepare what may be needful—I have a lengthy journey to take without delay.'

'Where, brother?'

'To Duglas, an' thou must know,' he rather testily replied.

'To Duglas!' cried Mistress Kelly, with upraised hands; 'thou canst never compass it!'

'Of that I have no fear. I know mine errand— God and His saints be praised! In Him I trust. "Strength will be given me even as my day."'

*   *   *   *   *   *

When Paul Balkason parted from Ayla he walked with rapid strides towards the road he had to traverse, not trusting himself to take even one look more at the weeping girl he had just parted from. Quickly he sped on his way, and, like the good priest, so deep in thought, unconscious of the gathering clouds, the moaning of the rising wind, or the brooding darkness that hung over land and sea; but while Father Kelly was oblivious of the aspect of air, and sea, and sky, wrapt in foreboding fears lest he should not in his life see his beloved chapel adorned as he so devoutly desired—Paul's thoughts ran riot upon battle scenes —where he was ever foremost and bravest in the fight —intermingled with gentler feelings as Ayla's tear-

stained face came before him; and again in imagination he felt her clinging arms about his neck.

'My beloved!' he softly murmured, and turned
for a second to gaze at the place in the distance where
he had left her; and as he turned, something bright
fell at his feet. He stooped to pick it up, and to his
surprise found it was the amulet Ayla had shown him.
He now remembered for the first time he had forgotten to restore it, and must have been carrying it all
these miles close clasped in his hand.

'Alas! how could I do this, and she doth prize it
so! I fear me she will fret and think it lost! But I
will wear it in the battle that is before me. 'Twill be
a charm, my loved one, to guard thy Paul from all the
arrows, let them be sped by ever such skilled hands.'

He kissed it as he might some sacred relic, and
placed it round his neck, safely concealed from curious
or covetous eyes.

*   *   *   *   *   *

'Tis needless to give in this short tale the history
of his lengthy walk, or details of the battle fought in
the Bay of Ramsey; suffice it to say that, notwithstanding the violence of the tempest to which he was
exposed, he arrived safely and unharmed in Duglas;
and as to the engagement in which he took part, do
not all who have written the island's history of that
period give full description of that famous contest?
What concerns us most in this story is, that Paul
escaped unscathed; but not so Dugal, son of Summerled, who, being wounded in the shoulder from an

arrow, fell thus helpless into the water. Paul saw, even in the thick of the fight, his vain struggles, wounded as he was, to save himself from drowning. What was it in his face that brought Ayla so forcibly before him, and by an irresistible impulse made him plunge into the seething waters and bring his enemy in safety on board his own galley? then see that he was tended, and his wound dressed and bound? Why? Ayla's eyes had looked up to him. Ayla's smile greeted him when in gracious terms the youth thanked his preserver.

Whom he had saved he knew not till he was told by them who were well informed :

‘ ’Tis Dugal, son of Summerled, Moarmor of Argyle; and this Dugal, aided by Torfinn, son of Otter, Summerled would fain make King of the Isles.’

Then he had saved the enemy of the good King Godred. Well be it so ! Would he have it other-wise ? No, *no !* he could not have left one so like his beloved to perish !

A strong friendship grew between the rescuer and the rescued ; but, alas ! poor Dugal gained not strength. Each day, indeed, he grew weaker; and when—as happened soon after the fight—a pacifica-tion between Godred and Summerled was arranged, there came to Mona Summerled's wife, a pale, sweet woman, who looked at and spoke kindly to all ; and she tended her son, with Paul and one of the good monks from Russin, who was well skilled in medicine,

6

but all without avail to save the life for earth—the soul was called hence !

One day as they watched, a strange look passed over the white face that lay upon the silken pillows; a faint voice murmured :

'My little sister lives ! I would fain see her before mine eyes close on all that now surrounds me. My sweet sister ! Go *thou*, my friend, and fetch her.'

'He hath gone in thought to the time when one (he must have been my Lord's greatest foe and cruel as the grave) stole this sister—a mere infant—whom Dugal, like us all, loved tenderly,' sighed the weeping mother.

'Nay, nay ! she lives !' again said the dying youth. 'Let me but once see her before I go hence.'

'He wandereth,' said the lady of Summerled.

'It hath been told me—or did my spirit, so soon to quit this body, see forms and scenes before hidden from my sight? I know not, but I pray thee believe me. Send, and speedily, for my sister. I would fain join Paul and Ayla's hands—they love each other.'

'Ayla !' almost shouted Paul in his extreme surprise. And he had never named her to Dugal. How, then, could he know all this? And she was, then, Dugal's sister—Ayla !

''Tis the name of our lost one, and of her he now dreams.'

'Dreams !' again cried Paul in excited tones. 'Know you this?' and he handed the amulet he had worn to Dugal's mother.

'Know it! know it! May God and our Lady help me! My sweet one wore it always round her neck. 'Twas once blessed, they say, by the good St. Patrick himself! Whence came it?'

'From Ayla I had it. Forgive me, lady! Dugal speaketh true. Knowing not who she was, I loved her, and she hath promised to be mine. And comfort thee, dear lady, about her, for indeed she lives, and is and has been well cared for. But she and the good priest shall tell thee all else, for I must haste. Time flies! and he who so prays to see her hath not long to tarry here.'

The lady of Summerled, forgetful of her dying son, rushed forward and held Paul by so close a grip he could not well shake off.

'She lives, you say? Deceive me not!' she cried. 'But tell me where—*where!*'

'Mother, let him go; 'tis all as he hath said. How was this borne in upon me? 'Tis certain not by spoken words. And yet—and yet—before Paul's assurance and his proof I knew this all. Let Paul go, dear lady; delay him not, I pray thee.'

So Paul, unhindered, sped on his journey. We will not pause to describe the rapture of the lovers' meeting, or Ayla's delight that the mother she had so longed to see was even now impatiently waiting to embrace her.

Poor Mistress Kelly, whilst busying herself in the preparations for this hasty departure, with trembling fingers wiped away many a secret tear.

'What marvellous events have come to pass,' she
said, 'in these few days! Ayla had ever the look
and ways of one who came of gentle blood, and 'tis to
me no wonder to hear she is the daughter of the great
Jarl Summerled. And he and our king are now made
friends. My brother in his old days gone a lengthy
journey! and still absent—alas! I know not where.
Ah me! what cometh next? My mind is full of strange
perplexity. What will we—Brian and I—and, indeed,
all here, do without the little maid we love so well?'

These broken sentences, at intervals, she spoke
aloud; the old serving woman her only listener, for
Paul and Ayla had gone together to Keeihl Vaayle to
offer up prayers for the future, and many thanksgivings
for their reunion when so lately they had parted full
of fears lest they should never meet again.

At last, all being complete for the young girl's
journey, she bade farewell lingeringly to the good
woman who had been as a mother to her, and with
many a clinging embrace and promises to return as
quickly as might be to see the friends who had been
such true ones to her, and whom she grieved to think
she might be long ere she could again see. Mistress
Kelly and Chrissie soon sat them down before the
blazing turf and tried to collect their scattered wits, for
such strange events coming into the quiet life they
had hitherto led, and following so quickly one upon
another, left them still almost in doubt as to their
actual reality.

And now we have arrived at the last chapter of this old-world story, and must as briefly as may be relate what befell the various people whose fortunes we have so far followed.

The priest's prolonged absence had caused anxious watchings, night and day, to Mistress Kelly and the good Chrissie. He at length returned, and, to their surprise, seemed to give little heed to the tale they had to tell of all that had befallen Ayla. After some slight expressions of astonishment and interest, he apparently banished it from his mind.

'Why, Brian,' said his sister, 'thou dost not care, methinks, about aught that hath come to our little maid! How is this—for surely thou didst love the child?'

'Love the child! ay, indeed, and truly! May God and His angels have her in their keeping; but I have now that in my mind and heart that leaveth no space for vain regrets or other thoughts. With Ayla all is as it should be. Now list, for I have that to tell that thou wilt scare credit. Thou well knowest how that chapel of Keeihl Vaayle was built—and yet how all these years I have waited and prayed for what is still lacked of completion ; and now God and the holy archangel St. Michael be ever praised ! all that hath now come to me—ay, all—all and more than one might think was needful to adorn the interior. . . . Nay, stay, interrupt me not, I pray thee'—for Mistress Kelly, in her amazement, had been about to break in with an

overwhelming number of questions as to how anything so marvellous had come to pass. In as few
words as possible the priest then gave the history of
his night in the chapel, of the intrusion of the men,
the burying of what he had feared was the body of
someone slain by them—then of his prolonged swoon.
' And thou wilt remember,' he continued, 'how Evan
Collett came for me to see one sick unto death. He
who desired my presence was Niel, of whom I told
thee. What he and the other (one Haco, from
Norway) had buried for concealment was treasure of
silver, gold, and precious stones.'

' Of silver, gold, and precious stones ! Why,
brother——'

Father Kelly held up a warning finger, which
effectually silenced his sister.

' This Niel—to whom of right belonged all the
treasure—that I may say Masses for his soul, hath
given it to me to do with it what seemeth me best. Part
have I put in safe keeping, or that which it hath
brought, to give to those—and they, alas ! are ofttimes
many—who lack food and clothing ; for the rest, it
hath got me all the chapel needs, the place I love so
well—so well, indeed, that ofttimes in my dreams it
comes over me like some glad assurance, that when
I shall be called upon to yield my soul to Him who
gave it, I shall be found kneeling before that altar ;
there would I fain lay me down to rest when death
comes.'

'Nay, talk not thus,' tearfully pleaded his sister. And as the priest was some while silent, she asked :
'But, brother, the other man of whom ye spake ; what of him ?'

Father Kelly's face clouded over for a moment.

'He hath, I fear me, passed away unshriven. He would else, doubtless, have returned for the booty hidden by him and Niel. He, ere they had gone many steps upon their way, would fain have returned and taken the treasure from where he had so unwillingly helped Niel to hide it ; and so grave a quarrel arose between the men, that Haco, in his wrath, drew his dagger and wounded his companion in the side. Niel fell, and Haco fled ; perchance he thought him dead. Niel after awhile essayed to rise, in hope his failing strength might carry him so far as to get to where aid might be given him, and in so doing fell o'er the rocks and got worse injury—the rest thou knowest.'

   *   *   *   *   *   *

Three days after the priest's communication to his sister the chapel, which had been for some while closed, was reopened for the celebration of the Mass. Great was the amazement of the worshippers, who had gathered at the priest's bidding, at the change that met their eyes ! The once rough, bare stone altar now covered with a cloth of richest workmanship, from which flashed many a precious stone. Gold and silver glittered in the sunlight that stole in here and

there through the narrow windows and shone upon
a beautifully executed figure of the Blessed Mother
arrayed in gorgeous robes, round her neck a chain of
pearls of untold value.

To all questions—and they were many—Father
Kelly deigned no reply, save : ' Would he, think ye,
who appeared to me, and bade me raise this chapel to
his honour, leave aught wanting to complete the
work ? Be content, therefore, with what thou seest,
and ask me not whence or how all these things have
been acquired.'

His sister he had bound to silence, and, much as
she loved gossip, she well knew when her brother
must be obeyed.

When next we enter the chapel of Keeihl Vaayle, it
is to witness a ceremony that was then, is now,
and we think we may safely say ever will be, considered one of great interest. A marriage is to be
celebrated between Paul Balkason, son of the Lord
of Skye, and Ayla, only daughter of Summerled,
Moarmor of Argyle. By the express desire of the
intending bride and groom, they are to be given to
each other in the Chapel of St. Michael, Father
Kelly being the officiating priest.

Considering the rank and birth of those about to be
united, the gathering at the wedding was but small :
The Lord of Skye (his lady had not come with him to
Mona, and still abode at home), Ayla's parents, her

three brothers, two maidens of high degree, of near kin to Fingala, wife of Godred—this same Fingala being daughter of MacLaughlin, King of Ireland. These, with some few of those who had manned the galleys by which the bridal cortége had been conveyed from Duglas, formed the whole party.

All were gorgeously arrayed in the fashion of the period. If we describe the attire of the bride and groom, it will, perhaps, suffice. Ayla, whose long fair hair fell unconfined far below her waist, had over it a veil that reached to the border of her upper skirt or tunic. This tunic, which came to her knees, was of a material much resembling in texture what we now call silk—the colour, pale blue. It was gathered in at the neck to a band richly embroidered with gold and precious stones. A girdle, embroidered like the neckband, encircled the waist. The sleeves of this upper dress hung loose and open from the shoulder, display-ing the under ones, which came to the wrists in many pleated folds, the material the same as the tunic, but white in colour; a long white skirt, which spread out far behind, was much like a modern train. Unlike present fashion, the shoes were of black leather, crossed with coloured bands of blue, and tied round the ankles like sandals.

Paul wore a cloak of cloth of gold, attached to the shoulder by a strap or ribbon sliding through a clasp —the clasp studded with precious stones; the cloak embroidered in red, the groundwork being gold in

colour. His tunic was of reddish brown, the shoes red,
vorked in with gold thread.   Upon his head a
' cornette,' or one of the round caps of the time, the
colour being red, the texture velvet.

In strong contrast to the gay clothing of the friends
and attendants of the Jarls of Argyle and Skye, was
the attire of the saintly Abbot of Russin, and his monks.
All were clad alike, for he and the twelve monks
who formed the community adhered strictly to the
example of life laid down for them by Conanus, first
Abbot of Russin—a life of mortification and self-
denial.   Instead of linen, they had garments of rough
cloth ; neither did they wear shoes or sandals, and by
their own labour won their daily bread, and, except
on lengthy journeys, never partook of meat.

What few of the spectators could find room crowded
into the church ; the rest had to content them by
standing in groups round the entrance-door, or else
raising themselves as best they could to look through
the windows ; but all were so quiet and silent, and
the voice of Father Kelly sounded out so clear and
strong, that those outside could follow the words of
the beautiful marriage service nearly as well as the
more fortunate who had been able to get within the
chapel.   Paul's voice, too, could be distinctly heard,
and even the bride's low-spoken replies.   Great was
the excitement when, the ceremony over, the whole
party filed out of the church ; and many were the
murmurs of admiration that greeted the newly-

married pair when they came into view. And as they at once made their way to the shore to re-embark for Duglas, they were escorted by a motley gathering of all the people round, young and old alike. Many blessings were invoked, and prayers put up for Ayla, who had been beloved by all; and when, ere she stepped on board her husband's gaily-decked galley, she turned to bid her friends farewell, the enthusiasm of all found vent in a hearty cheer. As it died away, the Abbot of Russin came forward, all making way for him. As Ayla and Paul saw him approach, they advanced to meet him, and, kneeling hand-in-hand, craved his blessing.

'Dy der Jee dou e vannagh!'

The abbot, placing a hand on each bowed head, replied, as they had addressed him, in Manx :

'Dy bishee jeeah shin!' (God bless and prosper you!).

After this, some more last adieus, and then the time came when all must embark. Mistress Kelly and the priest, who were to accompany the party to Duglas, got on board with Summerled, his lady, and the Jarl of Skye.

Poor Mistress Kelly, who had scarce ever trusted herself on aught in travelling but solid earth, was sorely exercised in mind, and, regardless of the ill-concealed mirth, instead of sympathy, her fears excited, deposited her fat person first on one of the soft cushioned seats, and then on another, as her ideas changed as to which might be the safest. At each

movement of the boat as it rose or fell in the slight
motion of the inflowing tide, she would give plaintive
utterance to some fresh exclamations of terror :

'Brian, Brian! had we not best return? O holy
Mother! Methinks we are over-venturesome to proceed thus to Duglas.'

'God send ye safe to dry land again!' cried the
anxious Chrissie, from the beach. 'Tar neose veih
shen' (Come down from there).

The men at last pushed out from shore, just as
Mistress Kelly was again about to change her position, and the poor lady's rotund person was at once
precipitated into the centre of the galley.

'The saints be good to me! this is a pretty pass for a
decent, proper woman like me, lying down from where
I cannot lift me, and a parcel of grinning men around.
Oh, brother!' she cried, as the priest came to her
assistance, 'I would give my best gown and hood
to be again by our own chiollagh [fireside].'

*   *   *   *   *   *

Many months have passed since the marriage of
Paul and Ayla, and they are now in their home in the
distant Isle of Skye.

Mistress Kelly, notwithstanding her misgivings, is
alive and well after her—as she viewed it—daring
exploit of going by sea to and from Duglas. She
and Chrissie are seated at a table enjoying a supper of
Braghtan barley-cake and home-made cheese.

'The jough [ale] is none so good as it might be,'

observed Chrissie, as she took a lengthy draught of the condemned liquid.

Both women had become quite used to the priest's absenting himself each night at sundown, and as he returned, as a rule, very late, they rarely saw him till the first meal the next morning. This night they sat long over their supper, discussing what to them was a never-ending subject of interest : the recent events of Ayla's marriage ; the grand feast in Duglas ; and all the gay doings there, of which Chrissie never tired of listening, nor Mistress Kelly of reciting.

Their solitary light, after spluttering for awhile in its stand, went out ; but the turf fire in the chiollagh spread a ruddy pleasant glow through the room ; so drawing near to it, they continued their chat, and were deep in speculations as to what Ayla's home might be like, and had just come to the conclusion that no doubt she was even now longing to be back in Mannin, when a faint sound as though someone had quietly entered, then followed by a heavy sigh, caused both women to turn hastily round, and there, standing near the table, steadily and gravely regarding his sister, stood the priest. Something in his appearance kept both Mistress Kelly and Chrissie silent, and, as they afterwards agreed, 'a strange fear and awe did possess them.' How long a time passed they could never say, till Mistress Kelly, in quavering tones, said :

'Why, brother, either we are late, or else thou hast returned sooner than is thy wont.'

The figure simply raised a beckoning finger, as though requiring his sister to follow him, then moved towards the door, and though it was fast closed, and so, as they affirmed, remained, disappeared from their sight. Both women involuntarily clasped hands in sympathetic terror, and when just then the door was suddenly opened, Chrissie gave vent to her fear in a loud and prolonged scream. Great was the relief they experienced when Evan Collett stood before them.

'The priest, where is he?' he asked, gazing in astonishment at the excited women. 'My father would fain see him. He is that sick and ill there must be no delay.'

'Where is he? Ye may well ask! In purgatory or heaven belike,' sobbed Chrissie.

'Ye fool, woman! Are ye mad? Tell me quick. Is he within?' And gathering from the confused answers he received that Father Kelly might be found at the chapel, he left them and hastened thither.

'I will follow him,' said Mistress Kelly, who seemed suddenly to have regained some composure. Not so the servant, who clung to her, beseeching her to remain where she was ; but her mistress shook her off, saying almost angrily :

'Thinkest thou I shall stay here when some evil may threaten my brother? He hath called me, and shall I refuse to go to him?'

And with wonderful firmness, considering her state

of inward tremor, she hastily donned her long cloak and hood, and made haste to overtake Evan. Chrissie, after balancing in her mind which was most to be dreaded—remaining alone or adventuring herself with her mistress—decided on the latter course.

The moon, which had not long risen, gave an uncertain light, as it was every now and then obscured by heavy driving clouds; but these soon parted, and the women could clearly see Collett not far in advance of them, but making such rapid strides there was small hope of their soon getting up to him. The sea now looked like a sheet of glittering silver, and the island of St. Michael, with its chapel of Keeihl Vaayle, for which all were making, stood out in dark and bold relief against the shimmering waters.

Collett had disappeared into the chapel long before the women could reach it, and when they arrived at the door both paused, hoping they might see him come out accompanied by the priest; but some minutes passed, and, neither appearing, Mistress Kelly summoned all her resolution, and, followed by the trembling Chrissie, entered. By the light from the many candles burning before the shrines they could see Evan standing motionless and alone. Where, then, was the priest? A nameless fear came over them, and both stood still. Collett, turning, saw them, and, hastily advancing, cried in agitated tones :

'Back, back ! come not further, I pray thee.'

Mistress Kelly, dreading the worst, did not heed

him, but, pushing past, made her way, followed by
Evan and Chrissie, to the end of the chapel. What a
sight there met her view! Her brother lay on the
steps before the altar, *dead,* his face composed, and
with an expression of ineffable peace. In silence,
motionless, she gazed upon him, and her mind
travelled back to when, years ago—ah! so many—his
face in life had worn all the beauty that it did now;
but, alas! the spirit that had then animated those pale
still features, and brightened the dark eyes beneath
those closed white lids, has fled! Once more in
thought she is a little girl running by the side of the
tall handsome brother, of whom she was at once so
fond and so proud. Then their home rises before
her mental vision. Yes, there stands the pretty
cottage in the shadow of the trees that spread their
green verdure over the roof. Beyond stretched the
wood where in childhood she had played, and where
Brian oft had carried her when she grew weary. She
could even now hear the murmur of the little stream
that ran between green banks, near the well-trodden
footpath leading to the village near. Then came the
day when she, with her father and mother, had gone
to the chapel to hear Brian preach his first sermon.

'Come away! come away! dear misthress,' im-
plored the weeping Chrissie.

She turned, with wonder in her gentle blue eyes, a
dazed look over all her face, and, submissive as a little
child, let them lead her away. The worst had been

spared her : a wound in her brother's side from a dagger-thrust, and from which the blood was slowly trickling, she had not seen.

*   *   *   *   *   *

It is a bright sunshiny morning in May—the hour, five ; and as it is a holy day, the sacrist of the Abbey of Russin has caused his beadle to ring the bells for matins. In answer to its summons the monks come from their various employments and file into the chapel.

Approaching the abbey is a narrow bridge, being only about six feet and a few inches in breadth, but wide enough in those days, when pack-horses were almost the only mode of travelling or conveying goods from place to place. This bridge has two arches, through which flows the stream that turns the abbey millwheel. Leaning over the side of this bridge, and gazing into the water that dances and sparkles in the sunlight, a figure may be seen on this morning, strangely out of harmony with his surroundings. His hair hangs long and unkempt at each side of his hollow cheeks, mingling with the matted untrimmed beard. His forehead is seamed with many a wrinkle, and from beneath his shaggy brows his deep-set eyes gleam forth with the wild fire of insanity. His clothes hang in rags from his thin figure ; his feet are bare. In one bony hand he clutches, rather than holds, a stout staff; with the other he is nervously displacing stone after stone from the wall of the bridge on which he rests.

7

Unheeded by him, the bells from the abbey ring out on the air clear and musical. Birds are singing their matin song, and the lowing of cattle in the distant fields, the bleating of sheep, with now and then the loud chanticleer of some neighbouring rooster, all proclaim the waking up of a new day with its duties, its pleasures, or its pains. And still that weird figure stays there, never changing his position or monotonous employment of casting stones into the clear water below. Hours pass thus, till again the bell from the abbey that has long been silent sounds out, telling all within hearing that it has arrived at the hour of eight, when prayers for the souls of the faithful departed will be said. This seems to rouse him. He raises his head in the attitude of listening, and, muttering something, draws his close round cap low down over his brows, and seizing his staff more firmly, starts with rapid strides towards the abbey, where he arrives just as the abbot and his brethren are again betaking themselves to prayer. He then slackens his speed and follows slowly into the chapel, and kneels down quietly near the door.

Many a wondering glance is directed at the strange gaunt figure, but he neither turns nor heeds, or, indeed, seems conscious of the interest he is exciting. After the Mass is over he watches his opportunity, and catching hold of the abbot's sleeve as he passes, says in a voice that rises almost to a shriek in its intensity :

'I deliver myself up for doing to death the good priest, Father Kelly.'

He was at once surrounded by the excited worshippers, who were ready to tear him limb from limb, so beloved had his victim been, and so truly mourned by all both far and wide.

At a sign from the abbot two of the monks went forward and drew the wretched man away from those who could scarce be restrained from avenging the priest there and then. He was safely conveyed to the abbey, but when questioned, all that could be gathered from his rambling answers was that he had stabbed a man called Niel. When he saw him fall *dead*, as he thought, a panic seized him, and he fled, he knew not where; that he fell and hurt his head. After that he lost all power of memory. One thought alone possessed his mind : that in some chapel great treasure of gold and silver was hidden, of which Niel had promised him a share; and now that he was dead, why should not all be his? 'But from place to place I wandered, and into every church that I came near, but my poor brain could not direct me right; but when I found myself at Keeihl Vaayle all came back to me.'

So far he had spoken with some coherence, but soon relapsed into his former disconnected mutterings :

'Eh! eh! don't ye see him kneeling there? It's Niel who has cheated me. He is not dead. Look at that chain of pearls and the sacred vessels, all gold and silver, shining in the light! Strike, faithless dagger! strike to the traitor's heart!' he hissed through his clenched teeth, and then suddenly relapsed into silence. His hand, that had been raised in an attidude of menace, sunk to his side. His head drooped. The abbot made a signal to those around not to interrupt him by word or movement.

'Ah me! that I should have done this foul deed—slain the good man kneeling there in prayer! What,' said he—'what gentle eyes he raises to mine, as I stand trembling—conscience-stricken—before him!

'"Poor wretch! what have I done to thee that thou shouldst lay this sin upon thy soul? Fly, ere it be too late, and spend thy remaining years in prayer and penance."

'Ha! quiet. He closes his eyes. He is dead—*dead!* No, no. Again he speaks. He raises his hands. Will he curse me? What will he say? "I have finished the work Thou gavest me to do." He sinks back again. He lies now where he first fell on the steps of the altar. His pure soul hath gone where mine will never reach; but—but—I must fly: said he not so? but where—where shall I hide such a load of guilt and misery?' And the unfortunate creature made a sudden movement as though to rush away, and when he felt the detaining hands of the monks he made one violent effort to free himself, in which he succeeded, but only to fall helpless on the stone floor, where he was a piteous sight to see, as he lay writhing and foaming at the mouth in a fit. One after another these seizures came upon him, till at last, utterly exhausted, he was as one dead, and in this state was carried away and put upon a bed in one of the cells. Father Angus watched over and did the best he could for him. In a few moments of consciousness he answered, when asked his name : ' I am one Haco, from Norway. May God have mercy on my soul !' Ay, poor sin-stained soul ! Ere morning it had passed away.

Mistress Kelly erelong partially recovered from the shock of her brother's death, and gathered great comfort by remembering and repeating to her sympathizing listeners :

' Did my sainted Brian not say to me that so well did he love the place, that it ofttimes in his dreams came o'er him as a joyful assurance that, when he should be called to give up his soul to God, he might be found, as he was kneeling, before the altar of Keeihl Vaayle ?'

THE MAGIC KIERN ROD;

OR,

CUR SHEN SHA IN GILLEY GLASH.

THE MAGIC KIERN ROD.

CHAPTER I.

The magic kiern rod—The heiress of Glen Auldyn—Her marriage
to Richard Clague—Richard meets a fairy who threatens
him—Wonderful effect of the kiern rod—Clague accepts
money from the elf.

IT is not only in these more modern times that the
Isle of Man could boast of heiresses, for we are
credibly informed that nearly a century ago there was
one of these *raræ aves* to be found in the romantic
Glen of Auldyn, near Ramsey. She was blessed
with good looks and pleasing manners, so we may
well believe that chroniclers say true, when they tell
us that many young men, needy and otherwise, came
from all parts of the island to pay court to the fair
Jane Clucas. Like the Lady of the Lea, however,
when 'asked if she would wed,' she, too, could 'toss
her dainty head,' saying—though probably not just
in these words—'Sirs, we would be free.' But let that
be as it may, she certainly preferred her liberty, until,

unfortunately for her, there appeared upon the scene a young man who was all that is prepossessing in appearance. Tall and straight, with chestnut-coloured hair and flowing beard ; such bright blue eyes and sunny smile, that altogether his attractions proved too much for our heroine, and 'in love fell she.' The successful swain, Richard Clague, came from the neighbourhood of Duglas, where he had been kept pretty hard at work on his father's farm ; and as work was a thing for which he had an especial aversion, he, on hearing of the fair Jane, determined to lay siege to her heart and possessions. She could not make even a show of resistance, and as she was an orphan, and had no near relatives to interfere or ask unpleasant questions, two months' time from their first meeting saw the fair maid of Glen Auldyn transformed into Mistress Richard Clague.

For the first year or so everything went prosperously, as a trustworthy man, who had lived with the bride's father, continued to manage affairs for the young couple ; but one day, returning from the fair at Sulby on a restive pony, and having, probably, had a rather liberal allowance of jough (ale), he was thrown, his head came into violent contact with a rough stone wall at the side of the road, and the poor man was picked up quite insensible and borne to his home, where, after lingering for a few days in a state of semi-consciousness, he breathed his last. Mrs. Clague took greatly to heart the death of her father's and her own faithful servant, and did her best to console his widow, who was now quite alone in the world.

Richard, though strongly urged to the contrary by his wife, determined to take the management of everything into his own hands instead of looking out for an experienced, trustworthy man to fill poor Ned Criggal's place. A year's intercourse had given Mrs. Clague a pretty clear insight into her husband's character, and what she knew was not likely to impress her with much confidence as to things prospering under his supervision. For the last few months he had been rarely at home; even the birth of a little son, now just eight weeks old, had failed to steady him, or keep him from his wandering life. Wherever in the island there was a fair or a sale of cattle, there Richard was to be found, coming home generally, after absences more or less prolonged, to his patient, long-suffering wife with empty purse, a sick head, and by no means an amiable temper.

Of course under these circumstances things could not go very prosperously, and matters progressed rapidly from bad to worse, so that at last the Clagues were threatened with an execution, or, as it was then and is now called in Manx parlance, being 'sold up.' Till now Richard had tried to blind his eyes and shut his ears to the true state of affairs; but he could no longer get money to follow his various pleasures, indeed, he seemed now on the point of being homeless. He, his wife, and Mrs. Criggal sat far into the night consulting and talking over what could be done to stave off, if possible, the sale of their furniture, and what little in the way of stock still remained on the farm.   At last, after various schemes had been proposed, and in turn rejected, it was decided that but one plan seemed feasible, and that was that Richard should try and induce his elder brother to lend him sufficient money to pay the most pressing of the creditors.   This brother had succeeded his father on the farm at Onchan, and, being active and energetic, was now a thriving, well-to-do man.

Richard prepared to start on the afternoon of the following day.   Things being so changed, he could no longer mount a sturdy steed, and ride where he pleased, but must e'en 'foot it' all the way.   He bid his wife and child farewell, and she and Mrs. Criggal followed him to the door to wish him luck.

' I must just get a rod for my brother's boy, Charley,' he said ; 'he was at me, last time I was at Onchan, for one.'

Having selected a stick to his liking from a kiern-tree near, he cut it, and, waving an adieu to the anxious women at the door, he started on his road.

' I have not,' thought he, as he trudged along, 'acted rightly to my poor wife.   It's a pity, just for her, that she ever came across me.'

He paused in his reflections for a moment, and for the time felt very repentant as a vision of the pale, careworn face he had left at the door looking after him came before his mind's eye; and then yet another picture, when first he knew her, bright and rosy, full of life and animation.

'Ah, well!' he said, 'please God, if I'm spared and helped out of this trouble, I'll try and do different, an' make up to her an' the boy for all the time that's gone in pleasures, an' drinking, and such-like— I'll turn to an' work, an' begin life again.'

'Begin life again, will ye, Richard Clague?' echoed a voice, apparently at his elbow. But as Richard looked in all directions to find the speaker, no one was to be seen.

'I was thinkin' that hard, I must have fancied I heard someone, for there's no one near, for sure.'

The day had been a misty one. And as it was the middle of January, and about five o'clock, the light was dying out, and Clague could not see very far before him. On each side were hedges of no considerable height, with fields stretching beyond; the road seemed, as well as he could tell, as he glanced from side to side, deserted save by himself.

'Yes, yes, fancy it was,' he repeated, when again the same voice took up what he had said—'Yes, yes, fancy it was'—and Richard, looking quickly to where the sound came from, beheld, immediately in front of him, and scarcely reaching to his knees, a man, to judge from his wrinkled visage and grizzled hair and beard, but not, apparently, quite two feet high. As Clague gazed in wonder at this strange apparition,

the creature placed himself in front of him, as though
to bar his further progress.

'Go back, Richard Clague, from whence you
came!' squeaked the pigmy; and as Richard tried to
proceed on his way, he began to dodge backwards and
forwards in front, evidently with the intention of pre-
venting him, and tired and depressed as Clague was,
he could hardly help smiling that so small and puny a
creature should think he could thus stay his progress.

'Now, now, my man,' he said, 'this little game has
gone on long enough; suppose you move to one
side.'

'Not for you, or any mortal man, will I move
where I do not choose to go,' cried the dwarf; 'so go
back to your home, your wife, and your child, Richard
Clague, idle do - naught as you are.' And while
Richard stared in amazement, the little man burst
into a fit of elfin laughter that seemed to be echoed
on all sides. Clague was no coward, but suddenly to
find himself—as he could no longer doubt—sur·
rounded by a company of 'the good people' was too
much even for his nerves; so pushing the creature in
front of him hastily to one side, with the rod he held in
his hand, he prepared to run from the haunted spot as
quick as his legs could carry him, when he was
arrested by a yell from the elf the instant the stick
touched him, and to his intense surprise the creature
fell to the ground, where he lay writhing for some
moments, apparently in great torture. Clague bent

over him with the intention of raising him, but before
he could do this the mannikin jumped up, still shrieking, and, giving one terrified glance at the kiern rod,
he cried in Manx, 'Touch me not! touch me not!
Cur shen sha in gilley glash (Give that to the Lockman),'
at the same time throwing a purse to Clague. The
next instant he vanished over the hedge and was lost
to sight.

With the purse in one hand and the rod that had
worked this magic spell in the other, Clague made the
best of his way to his brother's. Great was the
interest excited when, on his arrival at the farm, he
recounted his adventures.

On turning out the coins and counting them, they
were found to amount to exactly the sum necessary to
free the Clagues from debt.

Early next morning Richard mounted a horse lent
him by his brother, and with a light heart hastened
to his home, choosing, however, a different route from
that of the previous night. Quickly as he rode, he
found he had not arrived a moment too soon. Betsey,
her apron thrown over her head, was rocking herself
to and fro with loud lamentations: 'Och, och, that I
should live to see the day—an' the fines' bit o' lan' in
all the counthry roun'—ah well, well!'

The gentle, patient wife, tears slowly coursing down
her pale cheeks, sat near the open hearth, doing her
best to soothe the baby, whose loud cries added to the
general misery of the surroundings. Standing a little

removed from the women was the 'man in possession,' who, notwithstanding the wretchedness his presence created, was enjoying, with unimpaired appetite, a repast of oat-cake and cheese, and washing these down with copious draughts of jough.

'Cur shen sha in gilley glash.' To the delight of his weeping wife, Clague at once followed the fairy's injunction, and her surprise was great when she learned how the money had been obtained. Mistress Criggal, however, shook her head ominously, and uttered many well-known proverbs about the ill luck that invariably attends the using of 'fairy money' or gifts.

From that day Clague set to work in earnest to retrieve the past, and so successfully that ere long, by his industry and steady habits, he had won back all and more than he had squandered.

The kiern rod,* it is hardly necessary to say, he did not give to his nephew. It was preserved carefully in the family, and to some purpose, as will be shown in the next chapter.

---

* The fairies, it is said, cannot abide the touch of the kiern, or mountain-ash.

CHAPTER II

The unlucky fairy money—Betsey Criggal—The changeling.

IT is now six years since Clague was relieved from his difficulties by the fairy gift, and he has kept so steadily to work and to home, and been withal so kind a husband, that his wife—who has never varied in her faithful affection for him—has almost forgotten the two unhappy years of her wedded life, or has come to regard them as little more than a painful dream, best banished from the mind. But though Richard is all she could desire, and money troubles and anxieties are no longer felt, yet there is one source of sorrow and disappointment to both the Clagues and their faithful, sympathizing servant and friend, Betsey Criggal. Three children had been born to them—to all appearance, fine, healthy babies—and who, for a month or two, seemed to thrive, and gave every promise of living, when, without apparent cause, they would droop and fade away before their parents' eyes. Medical men from Ramsey, and Duglas too, were consulted, and prescribed to no purpose; and though doctors, as a rule, are never puzzled about the ailments

8

of their patients—or rarely confess to so much—yet
the insular Æsculapii had to avow themselves unable to do anything, and the babies were too young
for the usual prescription of a baffled doctor, 'Try
change of air!' And now there is again trouble and
anxious watching. Their fourth infant—a little girl—
is, as Betsey says with many tears and shakings of
the head, 'going like the rest.' There had been
great hopes of this child being spared to them, as
she was now six months older than the longest-lived
of her predecessors. Till the day of which we write
she had seemed bright and well. Richard and his
wife started betimes in the morning to attend a fair at
Kirk Michael, leaving the infant in perfect confidence
with Betsey.   •

When the hour approached at which she expected
her master and mistress to return, the faithful woman,
after hushing her precious charge to sleep, placed her
gently in her cot near the fire, and then busied
herself in preparations for supper, laying everything
on the table in the same room as where the child lay
peacefully and quietly, one tiny dimpled arm showing
above the patchwork quilt that covered the cradle.
Her preparations all complete, Mistress Criggal took
up a stocking she had been knitting, and with this
stood for a few moments at the door plying her
needles, and glancing now and then in the direction
in which she expected her master and mistress to
appear. 'They're late, surely,' she thought; 'but as

like as not they'll be gone to Misthress Kneale's—
they've been promisin' times to put a sight on her
when they'd be her way.'

About ten minutes more she waited, and then
returned to the kitchen. All was apparently as she
had left it, the kettle singing above the fire in the
wide 'chuilleig,' the large red tailless cat purring an
accompaniment. On the table the bread and home-
made cheese and jough, all ready waiting, and baby
evidently still sleeping, for no sound or movement
came from the cradle. The little arm had disappeared
under the coverlet, the only apparent alteration in the
state of things since Betsey had left the room. She
roused up the fire, and, tucking up her blue petticoat,
seated herself before the glowing embers, to wait with
what patience she might the return of her people
from the fair. Ere long she succumbed to the sooth-
ing influences surrounding her, and fell into a quiet
doze. The stocking on which she had been engaged
slipped to the ground, and presently she gave unmis-
takable indications of sleep, joining by vigorous
snores in keeping up the chorus with puss and the
kettle ! However, *she* declared after that she was not
'that soun'' but that any noise or movement in the
room—especially if near the carefully-tended baby—
would have instantly roused her; that she at once
wakened from her semi-slumber on hearing the
approach of the cart in which Mr. and Mrs. Clague
were driving to the door ; that the first idea she had

8—2

of anything being amiss was when she was startled
from her gossip with ' Billy the Lag '—who had had a
lift in the cart, and was giving her some of the news
of the day—by hearing her mistress cry, ' Betsey,
Betsey, come here, quick !' and when she obeyed, she,
like the poor mother, stood horror-struck and dismayed at the sight that met her view.   Richard, who
was just going round to the yard with the horse and
trap, threw the reins to the man standing near, and
rushed into the house, startled by the cries of the
women.   What was that piteous object that lay before
him—in the cot where so often he had gazed with
delight on his child, his beautiful, ruddy, bright-look-
ing babe, as she had lain in rosy smiling slumber, or
else with wide-open blue eyes, following the movements of all they rested upon : the waving of the rose-
bushes, laden with their blushing scented blossoms,
that peeped in at the window ; the birds or butterflies
that flitted hither and thither, or, sweeter still, when
those same looks fixed themselves upon his face in
apparent recognition and love, while his darling cooed
forth some song in baby tongue ?

The child lay where Betsey had placed her; but
instead of the healthy, chubby—indeed, one might
say lovely—specimen of infancy, that she had been
when put into her bed, she now looked thin, pinched,
and wrinkled.   Long skinny arms lay motionless at
her side, whilst the once sparkling eyes seemed to
have sunk into her head, from whence they glared as

if in anger and dislike at the trio who stood near, gazing in dire distress and horror at the spectacle before them. It seemed impossible to realize, and more like some awful dream from which they would awake, so sudden, so awful was the change.

'Oh, Richard, Richard! what can we do? Oh, my darling! my boggey veg millish! veg vien!' the poor mother cried in her anguish, as she tenderly lifted the poor stricken one in her arms.

'*Do!*' exclaimed her husband in agonized tones, 'do nothin', nothin'; there's some curse or spell upon us! It's that unlucky fairy money that I had to use. Och, och! a judgment upon me for the bad life I'd been livin.' But the Lord be good to us! what had you done, or the poor childher either, for that matther, that the like should come upon ye? Oh dear! oh dear!' and as he thought of the little creature he had left crowing in the nurse's arms, and to all appearance in perfect health, when he and his wife had driven away that day, and saw it now in this pitiable state, strong man though he was, he broke down utterly; whilst Betsey rocked herself backwards and forwards, uttering loud lamentations. What had so lately been a bright, happy household was changed into one of sorrow and deepest anxiety.

All night long the wretched mother, father, and their servant sat up trying all possible and 'impossible' remedies, but without avail. The child lay much in the same state, unless when anyone touched or moved it, when it would give utterance to a low snarling cry, and the eyes would settle upon whoever meddled with it with the glare of an enraged animal prepared to spring upon a foe. How could the hitherto soft, gentle blue eyes wear such a look? What agony to the watchers' hearts to see these restless orbs blazing like coals of fire in the dimly-lighted room, never resting long anywhere, but always charged with loads of hate and enmity wherever they travelled. And thus the weary night wore on, and a new day began, without bringing one ray of hope or comfort to the distressed household.

CHAPTER III.

The mysterious Irishwoman.

THE proverbial rapidity that attends the transit of ill news was not unverified in this case, for by early morning the Clagues' house was filled with sympathizing friends and neighbours, who all in turn offered advice or consolation. Conspicuous amongst them, not only from her extraordinary appearance, but also that, while each and every one suggested various specifics, this woman stood aloof, silent and motionless —a tall, gaunt figure. Her dark, deep-set eyes were fixed upon the sufferer. She was enveloped in a long cloak of some thick woollen material reaching nearly to her heels. For head-gear she had tied a handkerchief or shawl of bright colours under her chin. From beneath this some black locks of hair, slightly tinged with gray, escaped over her forehead and deep-set eyes. There, towering above all the rest, she might have passed for some fateful sibyl about to pronounce the doom of the little one, on whom for the most part her eyes rested.

In all the crowd none seemed to observe her

specially with the exception of Betsey, and as steadily as the woman watched the child, so steadily did Betsey gaze on her.

The sibyl—for so we may call her for the present—at last became conscious of Mistress Criggal's stare: slowly raising her eyes, she signed to the serving woman to follow her from the room. This Betsey quickly did, her tall guide leading the way with such rapid strides that the short rotund woman following found it hard to keep up with her, waddle as fast as she might ; nor did the stranger pause until they had completely skirted the buildings at the back of the house, and stood beneath the very tree from which, years before, Richard had cut the memorable kiern rod.

'Why, Misthress Ryley,' panted Betsey ; 'oh loss, I'm jus' kilt at ye—well, well — to—ugh—puff—to think o' seein' ye, afther all these years—loss save us—ugh—wondhers 'll never cease—ugh—ugh—no more 'n they won't—ugh—ugh—will I ever get the breath in me agen ? Well, as I was sayin,' to think o' seein' you afther all these years—yer an uncommon sthrong wumin ; but yer changed, changed terrible ;' and Betsey raised her eyes half timidly to the formidable figure scowling down upon her.

'And so are you changed—changed terrible,' echoed Madam Ryley, in by no means suave tones. Alas for the credit of the sex ! what woman, be she what she may, can take calmly any uncomplimentary allusion to her personal appearance ?

'An' where have ye been all these years ?' inquired Betsey, in a tone that reflected the huffiness of her companion's.

'Where but in my own counthry—Ireland. Were not my husband and my two fine lads drowned, in those cruel waters that are shining so deceitfully still now, in Ramsey Bay. Could I stay near to hear the winds howl above their ocean grave, or watch the waves pass over, either in fury or treacherous calm, the spot where they had gone down—down—never to gladden mine aching eyes with sight of them again ?'

'Ay yes, sure,' said Betsey, 'it was very hard on ye.'

'Hard on me, O God !' cried the woman ; but, suddenly changing her tone, she said : 'But enough of this, my good creature'—and, notwithstanding the incongruity of her dress and general appearance, there was something in her manner that seemed to bespeak her of a grade, in education certainly, and probably birth also, above her companion—'enough, I say, of me and my concerns—except this : that great kindness was shown me (the remembrance rests warm in my heart) by the father of the poor woman now in such grievous trouble, otherwise I had never set foot in this spot again, fraught with such sad memories to me ! There are those'—and here the woman's eyes assumed the painful glare, and her expression the look of mystery and cunning, that betoken an intellect unsettled—'there are those that do my bidding, and from them I have heard from time to time how it fared with the daughter of my true friend and her belongings. I should have come long ago to give mine aid in their season of trial, but I was warned not to do so; but now I am permitted.'

'God be good to us!' murmured Betsey; 'I thrust she has no deelin's with the devil or the little people!'

'What did ye say?' sternly demanded Madam Ryley.

'Nothin', nothin'.'

'Well, listen then while I tell you what must be done to restore to the Clagues their child—for that is none of theirs, but a fairy changeling. Do you understand?'

'Thè, thè [Yes, yes]!' replied Betsey shortly.

'Well, attend then '—for poor Mistress Criggal was trembling from head to foot, glancing here and there in the uncertain morning light, as if expecting to behold some ghost or goblin, or, at all events, some malignant fairy standing near.

'Oh, I'll attend enough; but could'n I lis'en to all this in the house?'

'No; where we are I'll say my say,' answered the woman, in the tone of command she had assumed from the first. 'As I told you before, that child is no mortal, but one of a fairy brood, and with you it very much rests whether the true child is restored. To ask the parents themselves to do what is necessary would be mere waste of breath, believing as they do, strange as it is, that the creature in the room beyond is their own offspring. Prompt and severe measures have to be taken, with no shirking of any suffering to the elfling. Do you listen?' she asked severely—for Betsey for some time had turned her head away, with her eyes fixed anywhere but on the speaker, whilst she kept rubbing one hand backwards and forwards over her mouth, her whole expression the while denoting anything but attention or willing assent to whatever Mistress Ryley might be pleased to propose.

'I'm lis'enin' enough,' she broke out indignantly; 'an' I'm wondtherin' at ye, or the likes of ye, thinkin' ye can teach *me* what to do. If the child is changed, as ye say, it is'n' to Irelan', or the likes of Irelan'—a dirt of a place like that—that any *Manx* body would have to go to larn what to do with the good people, nor, for the matther of that, for anything else, I'm thinkin'. The child is changed for sure—an' me an' a neighbour woman—a decent *Manx* body, too—is goin' to thry an' get the masther an' misthress to bed to-night, an' then we know what to do.'

' I don't believe even a surmise of the truth entered your mind till you learnt from me what is the case.'

' Mebbe not, mebbe not !' testily replied Betsey, her indignation getting the better of her fears ; 'there's no tellin' what bad things, shurmises, or the like, may come to them as is in bad comp'ny. But I can't be hintherin' no longer. I must go to see for some breakfast for the folks that's in, an' look to the cows.'

'Then go, you ignorant woman ; I must do what I can without your aid.'

'Ye'd betther not meddle nor make in what doesn' consarn ye, or lay a finger on the child ; ye'll get no help from me.'

'I have those to help me that you wot not of,' said the Irishwoman, in tones so grandiose and commanding that the good nurse's supernatural fears again asserted themselves, and she retraced her steps to the house in very undignified haste.

CHAPTER IV.

Different modes adopted to get rid of the changeling, and how this was accomplished—Conclusion.

THE eventful night arrived. Betsey and her coadjutor are seated within the wide open hearth, upon which a turf fire is brightly burning, and over this is suspended a large iron pot, in which is some mysterious decoction, that both the women are watching with great interest, each in turn giving it a stir with a long wooden stick cut for the purpose.

' An' how did ye get them to bed at all, at all ?' inquires the 'decent Manx body,' as she slowly works away at the uninviting-looking liquid.

' I toult them that if they'd jus' take a spell of lyin' down, they'd be the betther able to look afther the li'le [little] one, when I would be takin' a bit o' res' meself (I slep' whiles in the day, ye see). Well, wis that the masther, he persuaded the wife, an' says he, " Betsey," says he, when he got her out o' hearin', " I'll slip down to you jus' d'recly," says he ; but between you an' me, Mistress Cain, I'd putten something in their supper, jough that 'll keep them quite [quiet] a few hours, I'm thinkin'.'

'You're shockin' claver about herbs, I've heard tell,' responded Mistress Cain, looking with due respect at her companion.

'Well it 'ud be quare if I wasn', for my mother was wontherful for them things, an' her mother before her—'deed, there wasn' the likes of her in th' islan'; they'd be sendin' for her from miles roun' when anything went wrong with man or beas' [beast], an' she'd be curin' them mos'ly. Well, now you're wantin' to know what I put them herbs an' all them eggshells into yonther pot, an' the shovel in the fire heatin' at me an' all. I'll tell ye then, an' lis'en, woman ;' and as Betsey lowered her voice to a whisper, her assistant brought her head in close proximity to hear. 'When this here pot stuff begins to boil and to splutther, I'll take yon '—and a slight nod towards the cradle indicated that the unfortunate infant was the 'yon' meant—'an' put it sittin' near where it can see the stuff boilin': you an' me 'll slip to the doore, an' if then it 'll spake *words*, we'll do no more than go back, take out the red-hot shovel from th' ashes, put the chile [child] on to it, an' run with it out to the dungheap.

'Oh loss !' shuddered the other woman ; ' that seems terrible cruel.'

'Och, tut ! woman, don't be soft,' said Betsey ; ' it's not no mortal babe at all – at all. It's on'y—you know what wis'out my sayin' it; and then we'll get our own chile back again, sure enough.'

' I'm not likin' doin' it someway, though,' objected Mrs. Cain.

The two women after awhile became so engrossed in their talk that they were quite unconscious of the faint sound of the door, or even the breath of chilly night air that stole in as it opened. With all her wisdom, Mrs. Criggal had forgotten to fasten out intruders ; for in those days the Manx rarely or ever locked or barred their houses, the door being left ' on the latch ' all night.

The two conspirators would have been dismayed could they have seen who had come in so stealthily upon them—the tall figure of the Irishwoman, imperfectly revealed in the dim light. The fire during the cooking of the strange compound had burnt very low, whilst the steam from the pot filled the little kitchen with a dense smoke, through which the faint glimmer of the ' slut,' or light burning in a platter on the table, only indicated its whereabouts, without at all illuminating the surroundings.

Slowly and noiselessly Mrs. Ryley advanced till she had safely ensconced herself in the dark corner at the left-hand side of the hearth, between Mrs. Cain and the cradle where lay the changeling. Her eyes, that glowed and burned beneath her shaggy brows, seemed to emit rays of baleful light, were fixed upon the two women, whilst she listened, scarcely breathing, and with strained attention, to their plans. In this way an hour may have passed. Betsey ceased her low-spoken

communications, and, bending over the pan, said more
audibly in tones of suppressed excitement :

' Th' eggs is risin', th' eggs is risin'.   Now, Misthress
Cain, ye'll help me as I tell ye.   It won't be minutes
till all's ready.'

' I'm not likin' it,' whimpered the poor woman.

' 'Ut nonsense—lend us a han', will ye.   Don't ye
know it's no real child ye've got to do with ?   If I'd
a'-known ye'd a-been that tenther for nothin', I'd a' got
someone else to help me.'

' And if I'd a-known it was the likes o' this ye
were wantin' me for to do, I wouldn' a' come a foot
o' the road to ye.'

To this Betsey gave only a contemptuous sniff, saying :

' Now, ye fool woman, *do* ye know what I'm wantin'
ye to do ?   Jus' to give me a lift with this heavy pot,
so as I can put it where it will be seen by—well,
them as is to see it : then to come out to the doore
wis me.   I can do the res' without no help from no
one ; so you can go your ways home then.   Give us
a han', and make haste.'

Just as Mrs. Cain was giving her very unwillingly-
rendered assistance, Mistress Ryley turned to the cot
and began hastily and most unmercifully pinching and
slapping its unfortunate occupant, the poor infant
giving noisy protest in the most awful yells.

' It's seen th' eggs !   It's seen th' eggs !' cried
Mistress Criggal triumphantly.   ' Didn' ye hear it call
out " Take me away !"—as plain as plain ?'

' I don' know—oh loss, safe us ! this is terrible uncommon !'

' Didn' ye hear it call out " Take me away," I ax
ye ?' Betsey again indignantly cried, to her trembling
companion.

' Thè, thè [Yes, yes], mebbe I did. Oh loss !'

' Hoult on to the pot, then, wis me, while I——'
But what further Mistress Criggal was going to say is
lost to the world; for, to her and Mrs. Cain's dismay,
Clague rushed into the room carrying the kiern rod
that had before befriended him.

' Help me, woman ! help me, for God's sake !'
shrieked Betsey, ' or all will be spoilt ;' and, throwing
the pot down, both women ran forwards and seized
upon Richard, but not before he had time to place
the rod over the cradle, from whence these dreadful
cries still issued, accompanied by a sound of struggling.
While this is going on, a tall figure seems to rise
suddenly from the ground, and Madam Ryley stands
before the bewildered Clague, who is endeavouring to
release himself from the detaining hands of the women.

' Stand still, Richard Clague !' commanded the mad-
woman ; ' I will restore you your lost babe. Be quiet
and patient.'

' Quite an' patient, indeed, an' three women holtin'
on to me like this ;' for the Irishwoman had given her
powerful aid to the other two, from whom Clague
would have soon freed himself. ' Who are ye ?' he
demanded. ' I'm thinkin' I've seen ye before, some-

9

where—wheere I cannot call to mind jus' now, I'm that worritted with all this throuble about the child.'

'As I said before, *I* will restore you your child.'

'You, indeed!' panted Betsey; 'if on'y I'd a-got it out safe-t on the dung-heap, ugh! ugh!'

Meanwhile a dense and blinding smoke was rapidly filling the room; and while the whole party paused in their hostilities in the endeavour to breathe, a scream, louder and more piercing than any of its predecessors, rang through the room, and Clague's struggles again became violent to free himself.

'Let me go, will ye! let me go, ye devils! Lord! that I should be held in by a pack o' women! I tell ye I'll——' But whatever he was going to say died on his lips. There is heard the tread of numerous tiny pattering feet. Some figure at the same time softly brushes past the listening group. The cries of the infant suddenly cease. Again hundreds of light footsteps are heard, accompanied by a sound like the twittering of innumerable birds in spring, followed presently by the same heavier footsteps. The outer door opens for a second, letting in a faint peep of gray morning light. Then succeeds a dead stillness, till broken by a gentle murmur as of a baby just awaking out of sleep.

'Let go o' me, will ye!' again shouts Clague. 'Let me go to my baby!'

The spell that had influenced the whole party is broken. Richard is released, and all simultaneously rush to the cradle, and then Betsey turns to rouse the decaying fire. When light is obtained, who could describe the joy of the parents to see their darling restored to them (Mrs. Clague had now joined the rest). We leave that to the imagination of the reader.

All the various actors in the last scene took unto themselves the credit of having brought about this happy result with their spells. Betsey and her friend, the 'decent Manx body,' each averred that it was the sight of their extraordinary brew that had frightened the changeling away ; whilst Mistress Ryley affirms that had it not been for her timely beating and pinching, the ' good people ' would never have resumed possession of their fairy child, or restored the Clagues' their offspring.

Lastly, Richard positively asserts that he it was, and no other, that worked the charm by placing the kiern rod on the cradle ; and his wife, of course, as in duty bound, seconds him in this as in all else.

Where are there not to be found unbelievers? and there were some sceptics, even in those days, who were inclined to give credence to a story said to be told by a girl called 'mad Chrissie,' who it was stated gave the following version of the affair :

' She had been carrying her sister's baby, who had been left in her care, the mother having gone to Castletown to her husband's father, who was supposed to be dying. The husband himself was away at sea.

9—2

Chrissie, on the night in question, passed the Clagues`. and seeing the door open, and Betsey fast asleep, the idea crossed her mind of substituting her puny sickly niece for the fine healthy baby within, "to spite Masther Clague, who was always dhrivin' her off the farm." She afterwards was "longin' tarrible for her own chile," and watching her opportunity, stole in and again effected an exchange, whilst the confusion of the struggle was going on, and the kitchen filled with the smoke which so completely hid her from view She was so fond of the little niece, that her sister had always hitherto been able with an easy mind to trust it to her care.'

This story did not get out till months had passed. and Chrissie's charge was dead. When sent for and questioned by Clague, the girl denied all knowledge of the matter.

Of course all right-minded Manx folk knew that it was the work of the fairies, and Clague maintained to his dying day that what had upset their wicked scheme. and restored to him and his now happy wife their beautiful babe, was the magic kiern rod.

THE PHYNODDEREE,
OR GOOD-NATURED FAIRY.

THE PHYNODDEREE.

Glen Rushen and the tiny revellers—Glen Auldyn—The Manx maiden—The 'little man' and his unfortunate love suit—How he was changed into the form of a Satyr.

OH, merry were the 'little people' in the pretty Glen of Rushen ! How they danced and sang beneath the moon's pale beams, or under the brighter rays of the sun, or chased each other from one tall fern to another, playing hide and seek under the shade of the dark trailing ivy that spread its sheltering leaves over the soft green moss, from whence peeped out many a purple violet and gentle primrose, with here and there the starlike daisies that scarce bent their bright heads under the light tread of the fairy feet. Ay ! merry indeed were they, and fairy music and fairy laughter sounded out on the air, mingling with the pleasant ripple of the stream that took its sparkling way to the wide sea beyond, scattering as it flowed showers of grateful moisture to the waiting flowers that grew along its banks.

Amongst all the joyous crew one alone stood aloof, pensive and sad, taking no part in all the mirth and revelry. He was what might be called a giant by the 'good people,' being nearly two feet high, with dark hair and flowing beard. His eyes, that rivalled in hue the deep shade of the violets near, and his whole face were clouded o'er with melancholy. In vain did many a pretty fay try to lure him to the dance, or at least a game. He was not to be tempted from his unhappy musings, and while the revels were at their height, he had disappeared from among the sportive throng. When again we see him, it is in the first hours of the new day. In some mysterious way he has been conveyed in so short a space of time as from the previous midnight from Glen Rushen to the beautiful Glen of Auldyn, near Ramsey. Whether he had flown all those many miles on a bat's back— the fairy's favourite steed—or on 'the wings of love,' we are not prepared to state ; but this we can positively aver, that our hero was at those early hours standing under the blue tree in Glen Auldyn, and gazing with anxious, longing eyes at a cottage built under the shade of this tree against which he leaned. No sound broke the stillness, save the murmur of the little stream that ran swiftly on its course to swell the waters of the river Sulby, or now and again the faint bleating of the sheep on the hillside might be heard. Over this hillside, as the hours passed, came gleams of ruddy light ; and as these rays rose higher and higher, proclaiming the advancing day, signs of wakefulness were perceptible at the little cot. A tiny wreath of smoke curled upwards in the fresh morning air ; sturdy roosters

woke the echoes with their shrill cry. Presently the
door of the cottage opens, and a clear voice rings out
blithe and cheery :

> 'Oh ! Vollee Charane craad hooar oo dty Sthoyr ?
> My lomarcan daag oo mee :'

and then the singer comes into view—a pretty, bright-
faced Manx girl, and as she does, the watcher steps
forward and is met by anything but pleased looks by
the country maid.

'What ! *you* here again, little man ?' she cries in
angry tones. 'I want naught to do wi' ye.'

In vain the fairy pleaded as full many a morn before
he had done. Promises of untold grandeur or threats
of dire misfortune were powerless to move the obdu-
rate fair one to listen with favour to his vows of
love.

'Get ye gone, and let me never see ye more,' was
all he got for answer. And, alas ! his ill luck was not
to end here, for the king was so incensed at his
repeated absences from the fairy court, and, what
aggravated his offence, his daring to make love to a
mortal maid, that he not only expelled him from Glen
Rushen and association with any of his former friends,
but by spells—unknown, we trust, to fairies of the
present day—changed his appearance into something,
we should judge, resembling a satyr's, for we are told
he was suddenly transformed to the height and size of
an ordinary man, his body clothed with long shaggy

hair like the beasts of the field, and all his former beauty gone ! Misfortune, however, seems not to have had the ill effect it is said to exercise sometimes on the mind, by souring the temper and exciting un-amiable feelings towards those more happily placed ; for this poor fay, whose strength must have been super-natural indeed, used it always in behalf of those who were in great need of help.   The anxious, weary farmer has many a time had his heart lightened when he has risen in the early morn to see, perhaps, a field ploughed, or crops gathered in, or some other labour performed in a night, that weeks of toiling, late and early, with many to help, and consequently many to pay, would not see accomplished.   But woe betide him if, in gratitude of heart, he placed some offering for the kindly fairy, for from that day he lost all chance of his good offices.   Indeed, it is sometimes given as a reason why farmers of more recent times are left without this supernatural aid, that one, to·show his appreciation of the Phynodderee's assistance, left a gift for him of wearing apparel, and so offended was the fairy that he has never since mixed himself up in mortal affairs.*

* This account of the Phynodderee bears a striking resemblance to the ' brownie,' or good-natured fairy, of the Scots. —J. H. L.

CONCLUDING CHAPTER OF SHADOWLAND
IN ELLAN VANNIN.

:

CONCLUDING CHAPTER OF
SHADOWLAND IN ELLAN VANNIN.

In this chapter we give in brief some of the superstitions of the Manx not introduced in the foregoing tales.

The faith of this people in charms was boundless, and as they fully believed in the many ills that might arise to them or their belongings from the 'evil-eye,' where their own powers failed, they at once resorted to someone skilled in counteracting such dire influences.

In 1712 a woman named Moor, of Kirk Lonan, was condemned to thirty days' imprisonment, and on release was further punished by having to stand for two hours, enveloped in a white sheet, in the four market towns of the island—the reason for this penance, 'Witchcraft,' being placed in large letters on her back, that all might read. One of the many charges brought against her was that by 'spells' she had made the cows of a neighbour 'run dry' with

whom she had a long standing quarrel ; and though
the owner had taken up some of the soil on which she
had stood when 'casting the evil eye on the beasts,'
spat upon it, 'and thrown it over their backs' immediately the woman withdrew, strange as it may
appear, it had no effect in doing away with the mis-
chief.

These 'witches' were gifted with wonderful powers,
for not only could they by their spells prevent cattle
yielding the proper quantum of milk, but could also
control the winds.   A certain number of knots were
tied on a handkerchief ; this handkerchief being given
to the sailor or fisherman who had bespoke their
services, by unfastening one or more of the knots, as
might be found necessary, favourable breezes were
assured to them.

Some time about the year 1833 flourished a Mr.
Charles Seare, of Ballawhane, in the parish of Andreas,
better known as the 'Fairy Doctor.'   He was
supposed to be skilled not only in the cure of all
diseases inflicted on either man or beast by the evil-
eye, fairies, or witches, but was also gifted with the
power of 'laying ghosts.'   Once only do we hear of
failure ; the famous Buggane of 'Gob-ny-Scuit'
proved too much for him. The locale of this spirit is
now disputed ground—one history being that two
brothers were crossing Barule from Ramsey to Duglas,
each mounted on a strong Manx pony. Unluckily for
him, one of these men had his wife on a pillion behind

him. When near the summit of the mountain a quarrel arose between the brothers, and of so serious a nature that each drew his sword and engaged in mortal combat. Victory seemed to declare for the married man, till his wife, proving treacherous, threw her cloak over his weapon, when his brother, taking advantage of his disabled condition, ran him through the body. Ever since, at certain times may be heard, near the cairn on the top of the hill, a melancholy wailing, supposed to be the complainings of the spirit of the betrayed husband and brother, who thus breathes his woes to any who may adventure themselves within reach of the doleful sound.

This buggane is also claimed in Kirk Maughold; the mournful cry is said to proceed from a cleft in the rock, where there is a small cascade; but this being far too prosaic an interpretation, we shall keep to the first and more generally received version.

A twig or branch cut from the kiern* is supposed to be a wonderful preservative against the evil-eye and mischievously inclined fairies. On 'Laa Boaldyn' (May Eve), when all sorts of ills are to be dreaded from the little people, crosses cut from this tree are tied to the tails of the cattle and fastened on to the doors of stables and cowhouses. Besides this precaution, the gorse on the surrounding hills is set on fire to fright away evil-disposed spirits. At this time, too, there is always risk of the 'tarroo ushtey' (water

* Mountain ash.

bull) mingling with the cattle, from which very disastrous results in many ways may be expected, not the least of which is, that the monster tries, and often succeeds in tempting many a valuable cow to follow him into his favourite element, there to perish in the waters.

On 'Laa Boaldyn' children are apt to be enticed away to Fairyland, and on the last day of April anxious mothers might be heard calling their brood home betimes, by blowing, through a cow's horn, formerly the accepted mode of summoning the young stragglers.

To fairies, be they kindly or the reverse, is ascribed a decided taste for hunting, and the better to follow their favourite pursuit, they do not hesitate to invade the stables of any farmers near, and mounting their steeds, the unfortunate animals are returned in early hours to their stalls, but always with painful evidence of their hard night's work. If in the morning a farmer finds his horse looking utterly jaded, heated, and trembling, ' Ridden at the good people ' he will give you as the cause; and will then proceed to tell you instances of how he or some of his acquaintances have seen, in the night, little men dressed in the orthodox hunting-costume, red, 'tearin' over the counthrey' on their borrowed 'mounts,' 'an' little horns at them that they're blowin' in whiles.'

Of ' death omens ' there are many, the most striking of which is the phantom funeral. So real does this seem that, over the 'chiollagh,' many a tale is told of how, just before certain people have been called from this lower sphere, someone or other has seen a funeral cortége wind slowly from the house to the churchyard ; the mourners have been recognised by the watcher, and in some instances even the name on the coffin deciphered, as in mimic show it was lowered into the grave. This would probably come under the heading of second - sight. When anyone is ill, if what are called ' corpse-lights ' are seen to hover round the bed, it is considered a certain sign that the malady will prove fatal.

On New Year's Eve, in many households, ashes are spread on the floor from the hearth to the door. If there are indications of footprints, the directions in which they point is anxiously looked for ; if towards the door, it is an infallible sign that someone will be carried out. before the end of the year ; if the steps point inwards, a new inmate may be looked for.

On 'Oie Houinney' (Hallow E'en) many ceremonies are gone through, the more important of which may probably be considered the making of the ' soddag valloo ' (dumb cake) ; not a word must be spoken during the mixing of this extraordinary compound, or all the efficacy is destroyed—in vain will the maiden anxious in dreams to see her future husband place a piece of this cake under her pillow. As the in-gredients of this ' saddag valloo ' consist of flour, eggs and egg-shells, soot, etc., by eating, instead of sleeping upon a piece, she would probably under any circumstances have visions of many things she did not bargain for.

The 'quaaltagh,' on New Year's morning, is a person on whom 'hang great events.' Great uneasiness is felt in the household lest the first person to enter should be fair-haired, and, above all things, a 'spaagagh' (flat-footed) man or woman is deemed the most unfortunate—betokening misfortune through the whole coming year. One thing to be carefully observed on the first morning of the year is that whoever sweeps the floor must commence operations from the door to the hearth ; if contrariwise, all good luck flies the household for the next twelve months.

On ' Hop-tu-naa ' (Hollantide Eve) young men go round the country singing ' Hop-tu-naa, Trolla-laa,' etc., and expect to be presented with either money or something to eat and drink. On Hollantide Night it is believed that witches, fairies, and elves are allowed to roam about with greater freedom, and 'work their wicked will,' so they are specially propitiated. In most country houses, formerly, ' leavings ' of whatever had been the supper of the family was not removed from the table. Clean water was also put into crocks or mugs to refresh the ' little people,' before the household retired to rest. These same 'little people' cannot be thought hard to please, if they were satisfied with cold porridge, or even the more pretentious meal of ' braghtan,' which consists of barley cake well buttered. Between two of these cakes is laid mashed potatoes and salt herring, the flesh being carefully picked from the bone.

Though so considerately treated by mortals, to partake of fairy hospitality is dangerous in the extreme, showing that the good people do not appreciate as they ought the kindness shown them; and bitter experience has proved to many that to accept money, food, or drink from these sprites is always followed by misfortune. The dairymaid offers more inviting fare, with the idea of saving herself undue fatigue at the churn. A pat of butter or a piece of curd cheese is put within easy reach of the 'good people,' in the hope of gaining their favour.

On St. Stephen's Day a custom prevails which is not peculiar to the Isle of Man, though, perhaps, the origin there given of it may be. A fairy or witch, in the form of mortal maid of small stature but rare beauty, so bewitched the male sex of the island, from the eldest to the youngest, that everywhere might be heard wives and maids weeping for their false husbands and lovers. Farms lay untilled; fishing-boats rocked idly and deserted in the bays or harbours; but, worse than all, this siren led those of whom she had wearied to the sea, where they perished; and it seemed probable that the Isle of Man would not have one of the male sex left to show warranty for its name, when a knight, clad in glittering armour, appeared upon the scene, not only prepared, but able successfully, to do battle for the distressed damsels. His spells proved so effective that to escape them the witch assumed the form of a wren, and each year, on St. Stephen's Day, it is supposed she revisits the place where she had caused such misery. Hence the hunting and killing of the poor little bird, whose shape she is supposed to have taken.

'Jehaney-cheays' (Good Friday).—On this day no iron must be used for any purpose—even the poker is laid aside, and when necessary to rouse the fire, a stout stick from the kiern tree is used in its place.

'Laal Breeshey' (St. Bridget's Day).—Keeping this day has for long fallen into disuse, but formerly rushes used to be spread on the floor, and St. Bridget was thus invited to enter :

'Brede, Brede, tar gys my thie, tar dyn thie ayms noght. Foshil jee yn dorrys da Brede, as Chig da Brede e heet Staigh.'

'*Bridget, Bridget, enter. Come to my house to-night. Open the door for Bridget. Let Bridget come in.*'

This saint was born in 453, and it is said she received the veil from St. Patrick, and founded the nunnery at Douglas.

The Manx people had to contend not only with fairies and witches, but gobolds and cobolds. These creatures were supposed to choose as their home the caves with which the coast of Ellan Vannin is thickly studded. Like the 'little people', they seem to have preferred more solid food than the sweets 'the honey bee sips' from each opening flower, and the dew that hangs from its leaves was not sufficient to quench their thirst, for we are told they took toll from the flocks of the farmers near, and, besides this, milked their cows to provide for their wants.

At Spanish Head they deprived an unfortunate man of nearly his whole flock of sheep—they disappeared one by one—and he and his family seemed likely to sink into abject poverty and wretchedness, when suddenly the depredations of the enemy ceased. This farmer's son, who must have been a brave man for his time, made a search into the gobold's cave, where he saw the bones of many of the slain sheep lying about; but besides this he found a sack, on which in large letters was his father's name. This he put on his back and carried home. On being opened it was found to contain treasure of gold and silver. The ill-luck attending 'fairy gifts' does not seem to have attached to this, for this farmer and his family ended in being about the richest people in the isle.

The Manx, in common with many other peoples, hold a belief in 'cities under the sea.' These submarine cities are supposed at certain times to rise to the surface of the water, and if anyone on seeing this is fortunately carrying a Bible, he or she has only to hold this up, and they are at once conveyed in safety through the waters to these strange dwellings; but woe betide the unfortunate explorer if by any means he is induced to part with his Bible, for in that case

he can never return to his home or friends again.
Mermaids and mermen also find the sea and air of
this haunted isle to agree with their constitutions, for
the fair mermaidens are often seen combing their
tresses to the accompaniment of some seductive song,
whilst either seated on some rock or floating slowly
in the waters, her tail floating gracefully behind her,
and also by judicious management propelling her
gently on her way.

THE END.

Elliot Stock, Paternoster Row, London.